Fellowship Farm 4

Books 10-12

Melanie Lotfali

THE SNOWY SUPER-GLIDER-SLIP-N-SLIDER

BOOK TEN

NAW RUZ

The Fitzgeralds prepare for the annual Naw Ruz Mahta River Boat Race but there are some unexpected hitches. Skye-Maree and Olingah learn about loyalty and sacrifice as they work out how to respond to the challenges they face.

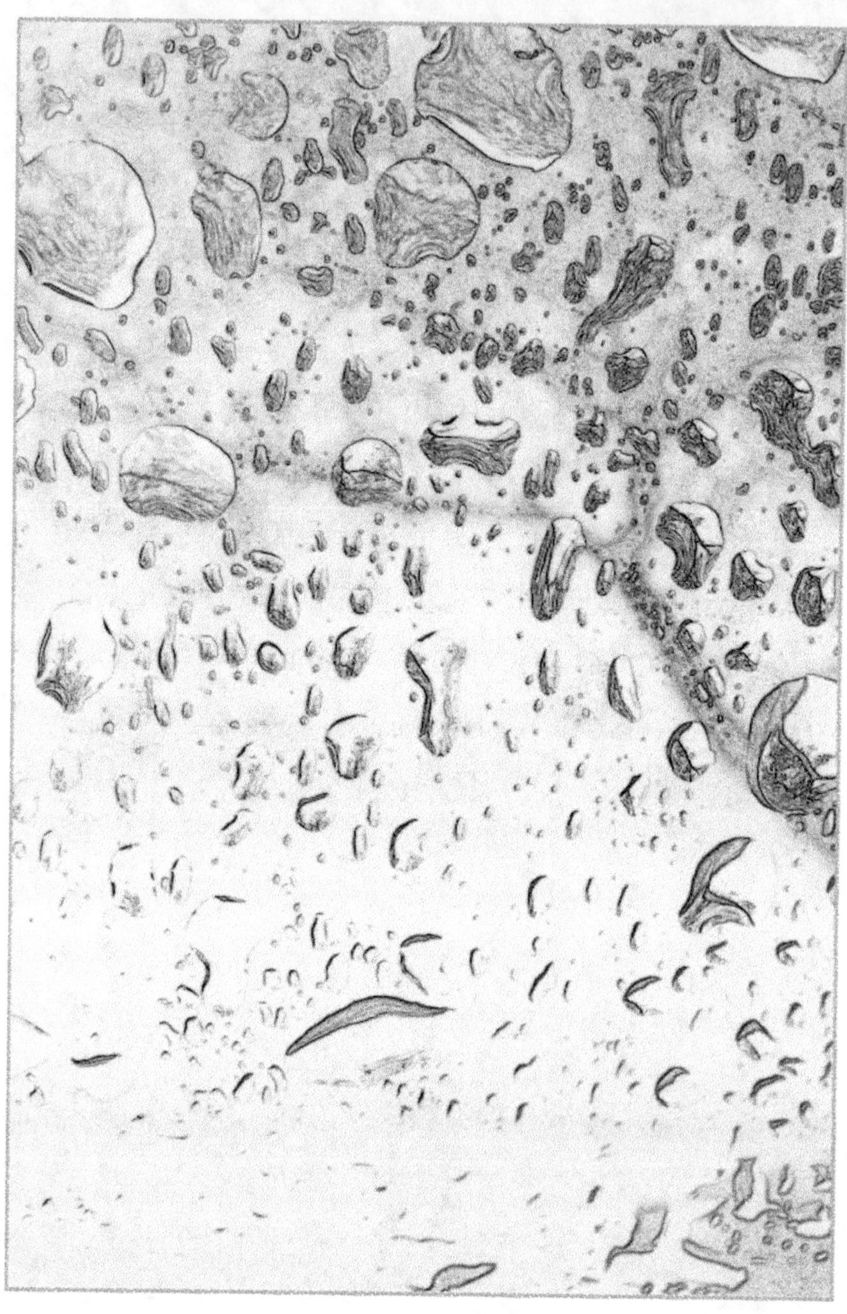

Rain

The Fitzgerald children woke in the early morning darkness to the sound of pouring rain. Leezah lay on the top bunk, for just a few minutes past the usual get up time of six o'clock, listening to the steady beat of the downpour on the window and roof of the old farmhouse. She smiled to herself. She hoped there would be much rain over the next twelve days. Leezah swung her legs over the edge of the bunk and slithered down to the edge of her nine-year-old sister's bed. Placing one foot on Skye's bed and one foot on their younger brother's bed nearby she rocked from one to the other saying, "Hey Skye, Olly, it's raining!"

Olly and Skye scrambled out of bed and the three of them joined their parents in the living room. Rommy and Flip had already had prayers and a big breakfast because it was the time of the fast. Once the sun rose they would not eat or drink again until sunset. "Mum," exclaimed Olly as he gave her a big morning hug, "It's raining!!"

"Wonderful!" smiled Rommy. She too was hoping for a wet couple of weeks leading up to Naw Ruz.

But the rain wasn't all good news. After morning prayers and breakfast the children put on woolly jumpers, socks, raincoats and rain hats to attend to their morning chores. As they did the rounds of the pigpen, the shed where the working dogs were chained, the chicken coup, the pigeons and the puppies, they shone the torch on the grass to try to find a path through the puddles and streams that were already, in some places, rather deep. The light of the torch reflected off the rain drops as they fell thick and fast from the slowly lightening sky. The drops looked like hundreds of beads of silver rushing towards the earth.

As the children reached the farmhouse the sun was just rising and the wind was picking up. They shook the water off their raincoats, hats and boots and hung them in the boot room. They hurried into the house to get ready for school, and for the bus which would arrive in half an hour.

By the time the bus arrived the rain had slowed to a drizzle. While they waited outside the gate of their farm, Leezah, Skye-Maree and Olingah gathered the brightly coloured autumn leaves that were falling in the strong breeze from the trees near the farmhouse. Golden yellow, deep orange, rich red: the leaves, shiny and wet, were beautiful. The air smelt of autumn too, the damp earth, the leaves, and even the chill in the air brought back happy memories of autumns past.

The school bus, clean of dust for once but now splattered with mud, came splashing up the road to the farm. Ms Rowbottom, the driver, opened the door with a lever. The children started to climb aboard. "Good morning," they greeted her.

"Don't you go bringing those leaves into my bus," replied Ms Rowbottom. "And take off your raincoats before you sit down on my seats," she added as the children abandoned their bunches of color by the side of the road, and then left their raincoats in the racks at the front of the bus.

As the bus drove from Fellowship Farm to Kellyton township it collected children from other farms. Soon the bus was full of Kellyton Primary School students. The windows quickly misted over and Skye drew a picture of a puppy, with her finger. Two other children played noughts and crosses on the windows. But most of the children were talking about the event that was coming up the weekend after next and soon the windows were covered with dripping pictures of rafts of all shapes and sizes, drawn with fingers in the condensation.

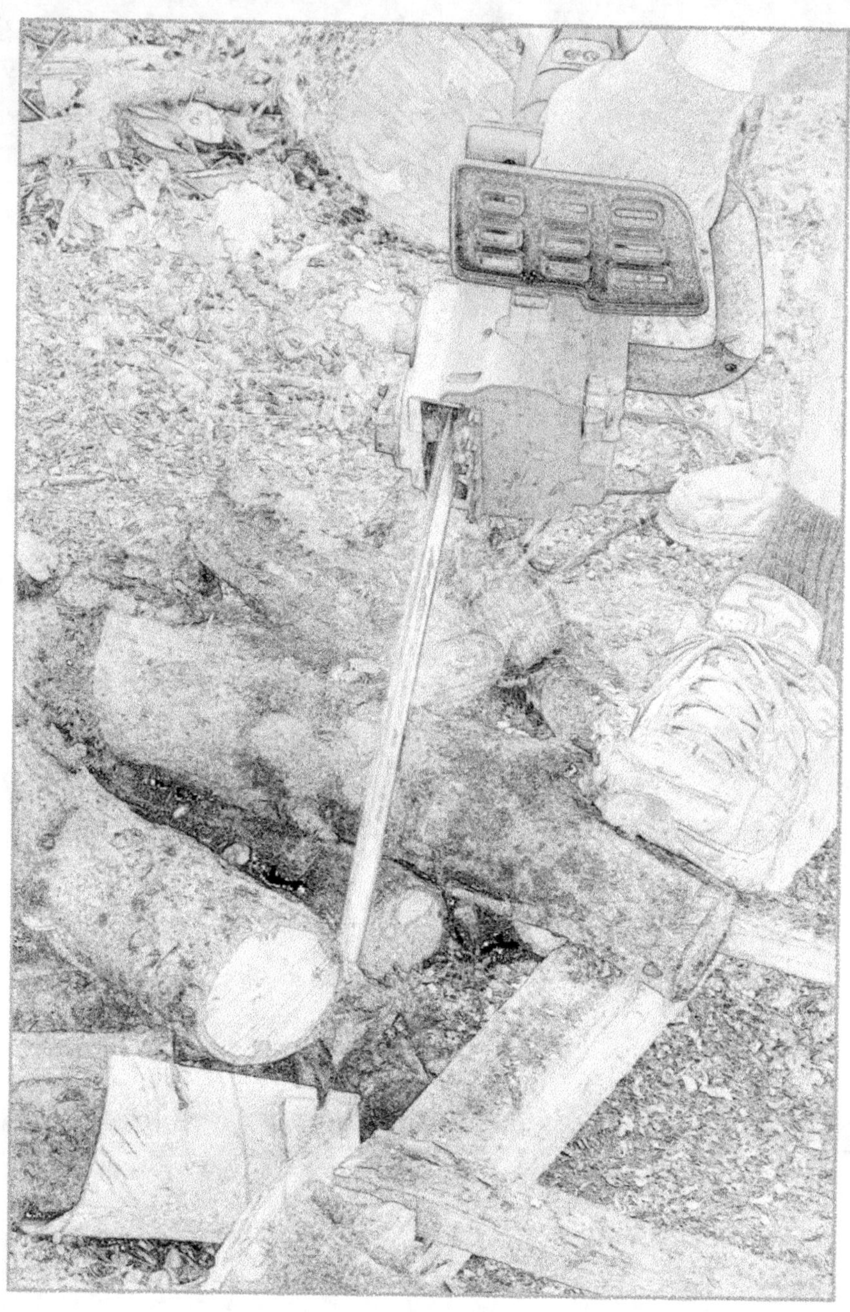

Preparing the bonfire

For the rest of the week the sun and the rain took turns in the sky, and the wind rose and dropped, pulling the leaves from the trees and scattering them across the farm. But on Saturday morning a bright sun shone on the green hills of the farm and the surrounding bushland. When prayers, breakfast and chores were completed the family put on their boots and gloves and headed up the slope to the shed where Flip parked the Ute.

The children clambered into the back and held tightly to the metal bar above the cab of the Ute. In the back of the Ute with the children was a large wooden box. It contained a chain saw, axe, hand saw, several packets of ear plugs, goggles and a can of petrol. There was also an old rusty wheelbarrow, turned upside down, and a big blue tarpaulin, folded and held in place by a corner of the wooden box. These were the tools they would need for the big job ahead of them.

As Rommy drove the Ute through the paddocks to the orchard and bushland that separated the farm from the sand dunes, the rushing air pulled the children's hair from their faces and put roses in each of their cheeks. When they reached an area of bush where there were lots of fallen trees and branches Rommy stopped the Ute. Sticks crackled and there was a scurrying of lizards and other small animals as the children jumped down from the back of the Ute.

Flip took the goggles out of the wooden box and put them on his head. It reminded Olly of his Uncle Jack at the Aquatic Centre and he started to giggle. Inside the goggles Flip crossed his eyes at Olly. Then he handed out ear plugs and everyone plugged their ears.

The task for today was to make piles of firewood. Tomorrow's task would be to cart the piles down to the paddock next to the house. If it wasn't the time of the fast they would have done both tasks today. But Rommy and Flip needed to practice moderation. They would not be able to eat or drink until sunset so they had to be careful not to sweat too much or wear themselves out.

There was work for everyone. Olingah and Skye dragged the large sticks and small branches into piles. Flip cut the fallen tree trunks and larger branches into smaller pieces using the chainsaw. Rommy and Leezah made piles of the wood that Flip cut, as well as adding logs that were already lying around. Sometimes Rommy or Leezah would use the axe or the hand saw to make a piece of wood more manageable.

At first it was very hard for Skye and Olingah to concentrate on their task. Every time they moved bits of wood they would find slaters, long fat worms, hairy caterpillars, coloured beetles, ants, lizards and spiders of various colours and sizes, as well as their eggs and other interesting things. Every few minutes Skye or Olly would call out, "Hey come and look at this!" Then the two of them would be occupied for several minutes looking at, gently poking or carefully holding whatever it was they had found. (They never poked or held the spiders!)

After about two hours, however, there were several large piles of sticks and logs spread throughout the patch of bushland, ready for collection tomorrow. It was time for a break. Rommy pulled out a basket from the front of the Ute. It had water, crackers, cheese and fruit in it for the children. Each of the Fitzgeralds pulled out a piece of freshly cut log to use as a stool. Bits of sap stuck to the backs of their pants but apart from that the wood made perfect seats

The fresh air and hard work gave the children big appetites and they were grateful for the delicious picnic. "I feel sorry for you," said Skye to her parents after a big drink. "It must be so hard to sit and watch us eating and drinking and not be able to."

"Sorry for us?" exclaimed Flip and raised his eyebrows high on his forehead. "What could be more joyalicious than being out in the bush with my favourite family, obeying the law of fasting of Bahá'u'lláh, and preparing for the celebration of the festival of Naw Ruz which we will have with our friends from Kellyton!?"

"Joyalicious?" asked Leezah.

"Joyalicious!" said Flip. "And how many of your school mates are going in the derby?"

"Lots!" grinned Olly through a mouthful of cracker and cheese.

For the past three years around Naw Ruz the Fitzgeralds had organised the annual Naw Ruz

Mahta River Rafting Race. Posters went up around town throughout the fast. The whole community was invited to make a raft or bring a rubber dinghy or a lilo and join the fun. The race started where the river ran through Fellowship Farm. It ended about fifteen kilometres later at the bridge, where the river went under the the road to the coast. After the rafting everyone would come back to the farm for a big bonfire and celebrate Naw Ruz.

That was why they were gathering wood. And that was why everyone was hoping for rain. If there was no rain, the river would be slow and shallow and the raft race would not be as fun.

As they ate their picnic the wind picked up and clouds scuttled across the sky. Their sweaty backs and foreheads cooled quickly and soon everyone agreed it was time to head home. Rommy and Flip draped the tarpaulin over the biggest pile of wood to protect it a little from the rain. Then everyone piled into the Ute. It was too cold to go on the back of the Ute now. No one wanted the wind on their face anymore. As they climbed into the Ute Leezah let out a big sneeze that startled the galahs in

the trees overhead. They flew off screeching
loudly.

The fair-square-share rock

On Sunday morning the Fitzgeralds loaded the Utes with the big piles of sticks and logs gathered the day before. Flip and Rommy drove the Utes back and forth from the bushland to the bottom of the hill paddock. Everyone helped to heave the wood onto the backs of the Utes, and throw, push and drag it off at the other end. By late morning the pile of wood for their bonfire was huge.

The family leant against the Utes looking at the pile, imagining the wonderful Naw Ruz bonfire with the Kellyton community next weekend. The autumn air was cool but there were little wet patches on the backs of all their shirts. Their glowing faces were streaked with sweat and dirt. "Brother and sisters," said Flip raising both his hands in the air, "Hi Fives all 'round!" Rommy, Leezah, Skye and Olly slapped his hands with theirs.

"Thank you for your service Mummy," grinned Olingah, slipping his small hand into his mother's strong brown one.

"No no no no no Thank You Olingah Giachery William!" replied Rommy, squeezing his hand. "Now who is going to help me make lunch, and who is going to help Daddy on the tractor?"

There was one last job to be done to prepare for the bonfire.

"ME!" cried Olingah and Skye-Maree at once. Leezah was feeling tired and was already starting to walk back to the farmhouse. As she walked she let out three big sneezes.

"Oh!" said Flip, "Everyone wants to help Mummy make lunch?"

"NO! I want to go with you!"

"NO! I want to go on the tractor!" Skye and Olly shouted over the top of each other.

"Mmmm," said Flip rubbing his stubbly grimy chin, "There's only room for two in the cabin of the tractor – the driver and one other. How can we make a fair decision about who comes with me?"

"Skye could practice sacrifice," suggested Olly

"Or YOU could sacrifice!" replied Skye glaring at her brother.

"Yep, you're both right. One of you could practice sacrifice. But if no-one wants to, how can we decide?"

No-one had any ideas.

Finally Olly said, "We could use a fair-square-share rock?"

Skye agreed.

Flip wandered over to the creek and found a small smooth stone. When he came back Olly and Skye turned around to face the farmhouse, away from Flip. When they turned back Flip was squatting on the ground. He had both feet and both hands flat on the ground. "Left foot," said Skye. "Right hand," said Olly. Flip raised his left foot and right hand for Skye and Olly to peak under. But there was no stone. "Right foot," said Olly. "Left hand," said Skye. Flip raised his right foot and left hand. "Yay!" squealed Skye as she saw the stone pressed into the earth where Flip's left hand had been. Olly knew it was fair but he was disappointed. He pushed his hands into the pockets of his jacket and pouted as he walked off toward the farmhouse. Rommy followed him. "It looks like you're feeling disappointed Olly," said Rommy gently.

"Hmph," said Olly. He wanted to say 'It's not fair', but he knew it was fair so he swallowed his words.

Skye and Flip climbed into the white Ute to head up to the big shed where the tractor was kept. "Can I steer?" asked Skye. "You may," Flip nodded and Skye climbed onto Flip's lap behind the wheel. Flip started the engine and changed the gear. Slowly the Ute started to move forward. Skye turned the steering wheel to the right so the Ute did a big half circle before crossing the creek and going through the open gate in the hill paddock fence. Skye turned the wheel left and the Ute headed up the drive way toward the tractor shed. When they got there, Flip took over the steering to park the Ute and they both climbed out.

Flip and Skye took a set of earphones each hanging over nails hammered into the side the shed, and climbed up into the tractor cabin. With a turn of the key and loud roar, the tractor engine came to life and soon they were bumping down the drive way high above the ground, on their way through the hill paddock to the bush.

When they arrived at the bush, Flip attached heavy chains to a big tree that had fallen over in a bit of a clearing. Then, with another roar of the engine, cracking of sticks and small branches the tractor pulled out of the clearing, dragging the tree behind it. Skye would have loved to climb down from the tractor to explore the patch of ground where the tree had lain. It would have been full of interesting insects and small animals. But it was not the time for that. She stayed firmly seated in the cabin, watching the tree dragging behind the powerful tractor.

When the tree was right alongside the pile of wood prepared for the bonfire, Flip turned off the tractor and climbed down to undo the chains. Skye jumped down from the cabin on the other side.

Unfortunately she landed harder than she had anticipated. With a squelch of wet earth she fell from her feet onto her knees hands and then face, biting her tongue in the process. Tears sprung to her eyes.

Flip still had his earphones on and was walking to the tree behind the tractor so there was no use calling out or beckoning to him. Slowly, Skye picked herself up, wiping her face on her sleeve and her hands on her jeans. She licked a clean bit of shirt to see if there was any blood. She saw a little patch of orangey red spit. Skye walked slowly away from the tractor toward the little bridge over the creek. When Flip glanced up she caught his eye and waved to him to let him know she was going inside now. Flip blew her a kiss and Skye moved on her bruised legs toward the farmhouse.

However, Skye was rather prone to accidents and was used to causing herself small injuries. By the time she reached the path by the farmhouse and then the back door into the kitchen, she was feeling mainly dirty, rather than hurt.

Rafterama

When Flip had parked the tractor back in its shed, he went back to the bonfire site for the orange Ute. He drove it to the shed and filled the tray of the orange Ute with plastic containers, rope and wood that were stored there. He drove it from the shed to the farmhouse and parked it out the front.

"Rafterama Supplies are in the back of the Ute out the front of the house," he told his children as he passed through the kitchen where they were eating, on his way to the shower.

When the children had eaten, they left Flip and Rommy dozing and reading in the living room and went out to get the supplies from the back of the Ute. They carried them around to the back garden where their curious six-month old puppies were keen to investigate and 'help'.

As soon as all the plastic containers, rope, wood and a few other things such as a plastic sheet, hammer, nails, tape and small saw were laid out on the back lawn, the children started to consult about how they would make their raft.

"Let's hammer the plastic containers onto the wood with nails," suggested Olly.

"If we do that there will be holes in the containers and water will get in and the raft won't float! Deeerrrrrr!" replied Skye rolling her eyes.

"Kindly tongue!" Leezah reminded her sister with a loud sneeze. (This was short for ' A kindly tongue is the lodestone of the hearts of men. It is the bread of the spirit, it clotheth the words with meaning, it is the fountain of the light of wisdom and understanding.' Bahá'u'lláh)

But after some time they managed to agree on a plan for building their raft and they started to put the pieces together.

As Leezah sawed the wood, she kept stopping to sneeze. She wiped her nose on the sleeve of her old farm shirt, until her nose was running so much she had to go to the outside toilet and get some paper to give it a really big blow. Blowing her nose made her head hurt and her eyes water. And her body was starting to ache.

As she came back down the steps to the lawn she saw Skye cutting the rope to attach the plastic containers to the wooden platform they were making. It was the last task and when she had finished the raft would be ready to sail. But Skye was cutting the rope into very short pieces and Leezah knew they wouldn't be long enough.

"SKYE! What are you doing?!" cried Leezah. "That rope won't be long enough! Now you've wasted the only rope we have!"

Skye jumped at the suddenness and loudness of Leezah's voice. Leezah was usually the peacemaker, the older sister who helped things go smoothly. It was very unusual for her to shout and to criticise. Tears sprung again to Skye's brown eyes. Olly was surprised too and his eyes opened wide. His tummy felt like lots of scared frogs were leaping around inside it. Quietly he said, "Sister, kindly tongue."

"How can I use a kindly tongue when you're wrecking our raft? I give up! You two make it on your own," finished Leezah and she turned to go into the house.

Olly and Skye looked at each other with wide eyes and open mouths. All the fun of making the raft had completely gone. They felt as if Leezah had punched them in the stomach. They were doing their best. They were all working as a team. How could they make the raft without her? They all knew that everyone makes mistakes. Why was Leezah so upset?

Sadly and as quickly as possible Olly and Skye finished off the raft. They gathered the tools from the lawn and put them out of reach of puppies and rain, on the verandah table. Then they went inside. Flip was asleep on the couch. Leezah was sitting in one of the arm chairs. Her face was flushed and she looked miserable. Her head was resting against the arm of the chair. Out of the corner of her mouth was a thermometer which Rommy had stuck there a few seconds before.

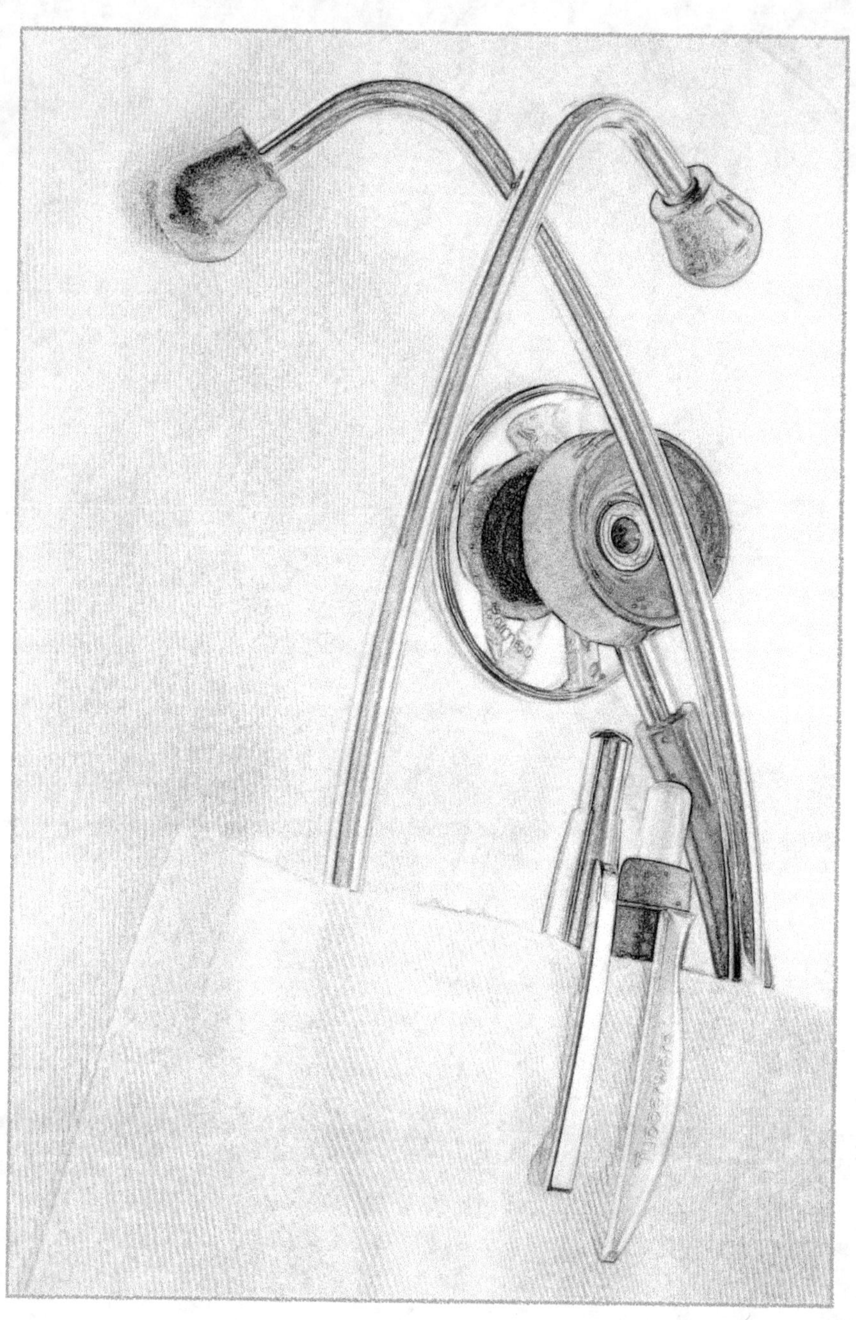

Sick and grumpy

Within a few minutes Leezah was out of her dirty farm clothes and tucked up in Flip and Rommy's bed. Rommy dropped a panadol into a glass of water. Leezah watched it fizz and bubble in the clear glass, until the tablet had completely dissolved. Then she drank the lemony liquid. Rommy left a glass of water and a box of tissues by the bed, closed the curtains, kissed her daughter's forehead and left her to sleep.

Outside the rain was starting up again and the sound of it on the verandah roof woke Flip from his doze. He opened one eye and looked at Olly and Skye, fresh out of the shower and in clean clothes, playing UNO on the rug in front of the couch. Skye looked up and saw his eye open. "Daddy! Are you practicing the Hidden Word 'Close one eye and open the other'?" She grinned. Flip opened his other eye.

"Where's my Leezah Begeezah?" he asked.

"She's sick," Rommy answered as she came into the room. "Her temperature was about 39. She's sneezing and achey."

"Oh no," said Flip.

"Do you think that's why she was so grumpy when we made the raft," asked Olly

"Mmmm, that's a hard question to answer Olly," replied Rommy. "And we just discussed that at the study circle with Sangeeta and Roger's friends last week."

Sangeeta and Roger had already completed *Reflections on the Life of the Spirit* and loved it so much they invited their friends to study it too. Now each week Rommy tutored a study circle with Sangeeta, Roger and three of their friends. "Let's get the book and answer the questions together for that section," Rommy added.

Rommy went to get the book from the shelf. She opened it up to section six of unit one. "Now, tell me, which one of these statements is true and which one is false: Conflict can be overcome with love and kindness."

"True."

"Words are more effective when they are said with love."

"True."

"It is all right to fight with someone if he starts it."

Olly started to giggle. "False."

"One has the right to be sharp with others when one is sick or sad."

Skye said: "False!"

"What do you think Olly?" asked Rommy

"False I guess. But Leezah must have been feeling so awful."

"Yep, sometimes when we feel sick or sad it's takes more effort to be courteous but we really need to try and practice it anyway."

Olly's thoughts suddenly turned to something that seemed much more urgent than courtesy. "What if Leezah is sick right up until the derby?"

. . . .

The next day the school bus left Fellowship Farm carrying only two Fitzgeralds to Kellyton Primary School. Leezah stayed snuggled down in the bed she had shared with her mother for the night. Flip had slept in the guest room. Leezah was feverish and aching and was barely even aware that her brother and sister had come in to say goodbye to her before they went to wait for the bus.

At school everyone was talking about the rafts they had been working on over the weekend. Olly and Skye enjoyed hearing about the fun and creative ideas their friends' families had. They hoped that Leezah would be feeling better when they got home and that the three of them would get a chance to join the raft race.

When they arrived at Fellowship Farm they crept into their parents bedroom to see how Leezah was going. Flip was on the phone to the doctor, making an appointment for the next day. Leezah was even more sick.

The meeting on Mt Carmel

For the next couple of days Leezah drank and slept a lot. Olingah and Skye prayed healing prayers morning and night for their sister. Skye sometimes wondered if the prayers would have much power. She was genuinely praying for her sister to be well. But she was also hoping that her prayers would mean they would all get to go in the raft race together. Finally on Thursday night Leezah came and joined the family at the dinner table. She just ate a little soup and toast but she was starting to feel better.

"How are you feeling sister?" asked Olly

"Bit better," said Leezah quietly after she swallowed her mouthful of soup.

"Will you go to school tomorrow?" Olly asked. Leezah looked at her mum with questioning eyes.

"No Leezah won't be going to school this week," said Rommy. Olly's shoulders slumped.

"So, will she be able to go in the raft race?"

"We'll see," said Rommy. It was the worst of all answers.

Skye then started to wonder about something. She didn't say anything straight away because she wanted to practice the virtue of tactfulness. But later, when Leezah had gone back to bed and Skye was washing the dishes with Flip, she remembered her thought and said, "Daddy, if Leezah can't go in the raft race, and has to watch from the river bank, do you think Olingah and I should miss it too?"

Flip didn't answer Skye's question directly. He said, "Let me tell you a story." Skye loved Flip's stories and she knew somehow the story would help answer her question. From the living room Olly had heard the magic words "Let me tell you a story" and he came in to the kitchen too, and sat himself on a kitchen chair to listen.

Flip began to tell his story. "Many years ago, in 1898," he began.

"Was that before you were born Dad?" asked Olly.

"Just a little," replied Flip.

"Shhhhh Olly," said Skye-Maree.

"Many years ago, in 1898, in the time of your great great grandparents, the very first Bahá'ís from the West arrived in the Holy Land to visit 'Abdu'l-Bahá."

"The West?" interrupted Olingah again. "Like the wicked witch of the West who was after Dorothy and Toto?" Olingah interrupted again.

"No my dear," said Flip patiently, "like from America and Europe instead of from Persia."

Skye finished drying up and pushed herself up onto the table next to her brother's chair.

"So, a long time ago, the very first Bahá'ís from America and Europe came to visit 'Abdu'l-Bahá in prison in the Holy Land. One of them was May Bolles Maxwell." Olingah and Skye's faces lit up. They had heard many stories about May Bolles Maxwell before.

"May and her companions arrived in the Holy Land after a long and difficult journey. They took a small boat in a rough and stormy sea to get to Haifa. And then they went by horse and carriage along the sea shore to get to Akka. Finally after many months of wishing and hoping for that moment, they got to meet 'Abdu'l-Bahá. Their hearts were full of joy.

"'Abdu'l-Bahá told the pilgrims that on Sunday He would meet them on Mount Carmel, under the shade of the trees where Bahá'u'lláh had rested when He was still alive. Everyone was really looking forward to it, especially May. But then, on Sunday morning May woke up feeling very very sick.

"She thought she would miss out on the visit to Mount Carmel with the Master. She felt very sad. The other pilgrims felt sorry for her but they got ready to go. Then, 'Abdu'l-Bahá arrived at the bedside of May Maxwell. He felt her pulse and said: 'There will be no meeting on Mount Carmel to-day. We could not go and leave one of the beloved of God alone and sick. We could none of us be happy unless all the beloved were happy.'

"Everyone was very surprised. Just because one person was sick the whole gathering was cancelled. They realised that no matter how important the meeting was, it was much more important to show love and kindness to all the friends. And so, the meeting on Mount Carmel with 'Abdu'l-Bahá waited for another day."

Skye knew she had the answer to her question. She just had to wait and see how Leezah would be feeling on Saturday.

47

WELCOME TO THE
NAIV RUZ
MAHTA RIVER
RAFTING RACE

Raising the banner

When Olly and Skye arrived home on the school bus they were very happy to see Leezah at the gate. She was rugged up in a big woolly jumper and coat with a warm hat pulled over her ears and in her hands were bunches of richly colored autumn leaves. After climbing out of the bus they gave her a big hug.

"Sister!" exclaimed Olly. "Are you better?"

"Well, today was the Boring Day!" replied Leezah. Olly and Skye knew what she meant. Whenever they fell sick there were days of being sick and then when they were well again there were days of being well and in between was the Boring Day where they were too weak to go to school or go out and play, but too well to just lie around in bed all day.

"Yay!" said Skye. "That means tomorrow you will be well again."

Olly and Skye changed quickly out of their school uniforms and into their farm clothes. They ate the snack that Flip had prepared for them. Just as they finished their juice there was a honk out the front of the farmhouse. The three children hurried out the back door and pulled on their boots from the boot room. They ran around to the front of the house and clambered into the cabin of the Ute. Flip would need to drive on the public road for a kilometre or two so they couldn't go in the back. For the first time in days it didn't hurt Leezah's head to walk and run.

Flip drove slowly out of the farm and turned left toward the coast. Every now and then he stopped the Ute and one of the children hopped out and stuck an orange flag into the gravel on the side of the road. Soon Flip turned right into the paddock that lead to the river. The children continued to leave the orange flags along the side of the road until they reached the open grassy patch by the river bank where people would park their cars when they arrived for the race.

He pulled up under a big old gum tree. A flock of parakeets flew swiftly into the air. The children climbed out and undid the back of the Ute tray. They pulled out a big canvas banner with four ropes attached – one to each corner. It was the same banner they had used before. Uncle Jack had helped them make it for the first year. The banner said:

Welcome to the Naw Ruz
Mahta River Rafting Race

Olly clambered up one of the gum trees on the river bank slipping and sliding on the smooth white bark between branches. Skye climbed one a few metres away and Flip passed them the ropes to loop over the branches. Soon the banner was hanging between the trees. It was a little crooked and when strong gusts of wind blew it was hard to read the letters on the flapping canvas. But it was up, ready for the big race the next day.

Leezah checked the level of the river and saw that it was flowing solidly. It would be a good derby tomorrow. She helped clear some branches away from the area where people would park their cars. After picking up a few branches though, her head started to hurt and she climbed into the back of the Ute to rest. Olly and Skye climbed out of the trees and went over the where their sister sat. "Are you okay?" said Skye

"Yup," said Leezah softly.

Skye and Olly looked at each other. The race was only 24 hours away. They thought of the raft they had made. They thought of the fun they had had the years before, racing down the river with their friends, more in the water than on it, most of the time. And they thought of 'Abdu'l-Bahá and May Maxwell.

After preparing the river side, the children and Flip returned to the farmhouse to prepare for the nineteen day feast. But only Olly and Skye-Maree put their feast clothes on. Leezah put her pajamas on and climbed into bed. "I'll stay with Leezah," said Rommy to Flip.

"Okay my love," said Flip giving her a kiss on the cheek. "I'll take these angels off to be 'spiritually restored' and 'endued with a power that is not of this world'. Olly looked at Flip in confusion. "What are you talking about Daddy?"

"It means I am taking you to feast possum," said Flip.

"Oh," said Olly, not really sure what his dad was talking about. Then he turned to his mum.

"Do you think Leezah will be well by tomorrow morning Mummy?"

"I really don't know Olly. Maybe she just needs one more big sleep. Or maybe ...that won't be enough."

The derby and possum poo

Naw Ruz dawned bright, sunny and warm. The whole family slept later than usual, tired from the early mornings of the fast and the late night of the feast. When Olly opened his eyes in the sunlit bedroom and uncurled himself like wombat from his burrow of doona, he saw that Skye-Maree was awake and looking at him. Both of them were thinking the same thing. Both of them wondered if their family was going to be able to participate in the derby.

Two brown legs swinging over the side of the top bunk was the first good sign. A big smile on Leezah's face was the second good sign. But the best of all was when she leapt onto her brother's bed and tackled him, with all her usual energy, rolling him up in his doona and roaring like a lion. In seconds Skye was on her back, rescuing her brother from the fierce beast and then being tickled herself. "Yay!!" came an excited but muffled voice from under the doona. "She's better!"

Prayers, breakfast and chores were rushed affairs. Just as the children hurried back to the house after feeding the pigs, dogs, hens and pigeons, the first cars appeared in the distance coming up the long straight stretch of dirt road from Kellyton toward Fellowship Farm.

"They're coming!!" screeched Olly and they all broke into a run, up the veranda steps.

Soon the Fitzgerald family had piled into the Ute, with the children's raft and a rubber dinghy tied securely on the tray at the back and were following their own trail of orange flags toward the river. As they untied their rafts other cars began to arrive. Soon the field by the river was full of cars, colourful rafts, people in swimmers, as well as floaties and lifejackets, hats, gumboots and zinc cream. It was perfect weather: Hot and still. The children were keen to get in the river and soon it was full of rafts of different shapes, sizes and stability, covered in wet, laughing and splashing families, struggling to get on, stay on and float.

At ten o'clock Rommy officially welcomed the Kellyton community to the annual Naw Ruz derby. She then cried: On your marks. Get set. GO! before splashing into the water herself and joining Flip in their rubber dinghy. Leezah, Skye and Olly, like most of the other contestants, tumbled on and off their sagging and disintegrating raft and with great hilarity they all headed off downstream.

Very few rafts made it all the way to the bridge in one piece and by the end of the race the main task was to catch the bits of wood, foam, plastic containers, balloon and other things that were floating freely down the river toward the bridge. It was, as always, rather unclear who won the derby and so Rommy and Flip declared them all winners. The rafts and lilos, rubber dinghies and various bits and pieces were pulled from the river. A few adults who had not gone in the race met everyone at the bridge to cart Ute loads of wet and laughing Kellytonians back to the start to collect their vehicles.

Soon after this, the stream of cars and Utes flowed from the river bank to the field behind the farmhouse. As the community gathered around and the barbecue was started, Rommy lit the bonfire and soon it was a roaring, hissing, crackling, tower of flame and smoke, drying the damp wood and exciting the children.

The air filled with the smell of barbecuing veggie burgers, sausages and onions. After the children had several rounds of tip around the bonfire, Flip announced that the food was ready. To Leezah's embarrassment he did this with a long loud blast on his imaginary trumpet.

"De de-de-de De de-de-de De de-de-de DE!"

A long line of hungry children appeared at the barbecue who were soon happily burning their tongues on hot burgers and sausages wrapped in bread and tomato sauce.

And then the hunt for good marshmallow sticks began. Big bags of marshmallows were handed around and soon there were blobs of melting pink sugar dripping into the flames at the edge of the bonfire and into eager little mouths.

When everyone had full and bursting tummies, Flip announced the start of the scavenger hunt. He handed out the lists of things to find and the children scattered over the field searching for live worms, possum poo, a yellow flower, a stick that looked like an animal and many other treasures.

"Possum poo!?" exclaimed Leezah as she read the list to some younger children who couldn't read the long words. "That's disgusting!" But her group went off none the less to see what 'treasure' they would find. It was Skye's group who came up with the creative idea of carrying the possum poo on a leaf!

A Naw Ruz resolution

Piles of treasure were brought to Flip to inspect; leftover sausages – now cold – were eaten; and the bonfire settled to a low smoldering pile of ash. Tired children sat with their parents in the grass by the fire, heads resting on the legs of mummies and daddies. Gradually, one by one, families gathered their belongings, thanked the Fitzgeralds for another wonderful Naw Ruz, and headed to their cars.

Olly, Leezah and Skye-Maree were tired and grubby. Particularly Skye seemed covered from head to toe with sticky marshmallow, sausage grease, and charcoal streaks. Her knees were muddy and her hair was a wild tangle filled with bits of stick and leaves from the river. With the last of their energy they helped Rommy and Flip pack up the barbecue and take the plastic cups and plates inside for washing. Flip made sure the bonfire was completely out and then joined them inside.

"Thank you for a wonderful Naw Ruz," said Leezah wrapping her arms around Rommy.

"Yes, thank you," added Skye and Olly hugging their dad.

"No no no no no no no, thank YOU!" said Flip, "For your helpfulness, joyfulness, gratitude and welcomefulness."

"Welcomefulness?" asked Skye.

"Yes you made all our guests feel very welcome. Welcomeful-ness is the virtue of making people feel welcome, don't you know?"

Olly wasn't sure if that was really true. Sometimes his dad seemed to know words of which no-one else in the world had ever heard.

"Did anyone ask about the meaning of Naw Ruz this year?" asked Leezah.

"Yes," said Rommy happily. I had a long talk with Julie from the library and she is keen to come to our next Devotional Meeting.

"One of my friends asked too," said Leezah. "I think we could invite her to the children's class."

"Maybe it's time we got a junior youth group together for you and your friends Leezah?"

"Yes!" said Leezah. She had really outgrown the children's class and was starting to find it rather boring.

"The only problem," added Rommy, "is that if we start it now it will be interrupted next year when you go to boarding school for high school."

Leezah's tummy did a quick flip. She didn't like to think about the next school year, when she would have to go all the way to Launceston and stay there during term. She decided not to think about it. After all, it was a whole year away.

"Well, maybe we can start it this year and just see what happens next year?"

"Good idea," said Rommy. "Let's make that our New Year's resolution: to establish a Junior Youth Group at Fellowship Farm."

"An excellent idea," exclaimed Flip. "Happy Naw Ruz!"

"Happy Naw Ruz," replied the Fitzgeralds of Fellowship Farm.

BOOK ELEVEN

SKIING THE SLOPES

The Fitzgerald family rug up and head for the ski slopes in this the eleventh book in the Fellowship Farm series. Along they way they experience the life-threatening danger of losing unity, the challenge of learning to ski, the power of prayer, and patience in the face of frustration. They meet funny Magic, the back to front Panda, and suffer some bruises Their patience is well rewarded when their parents announce that a dear wish of the children is to be fulfilled.

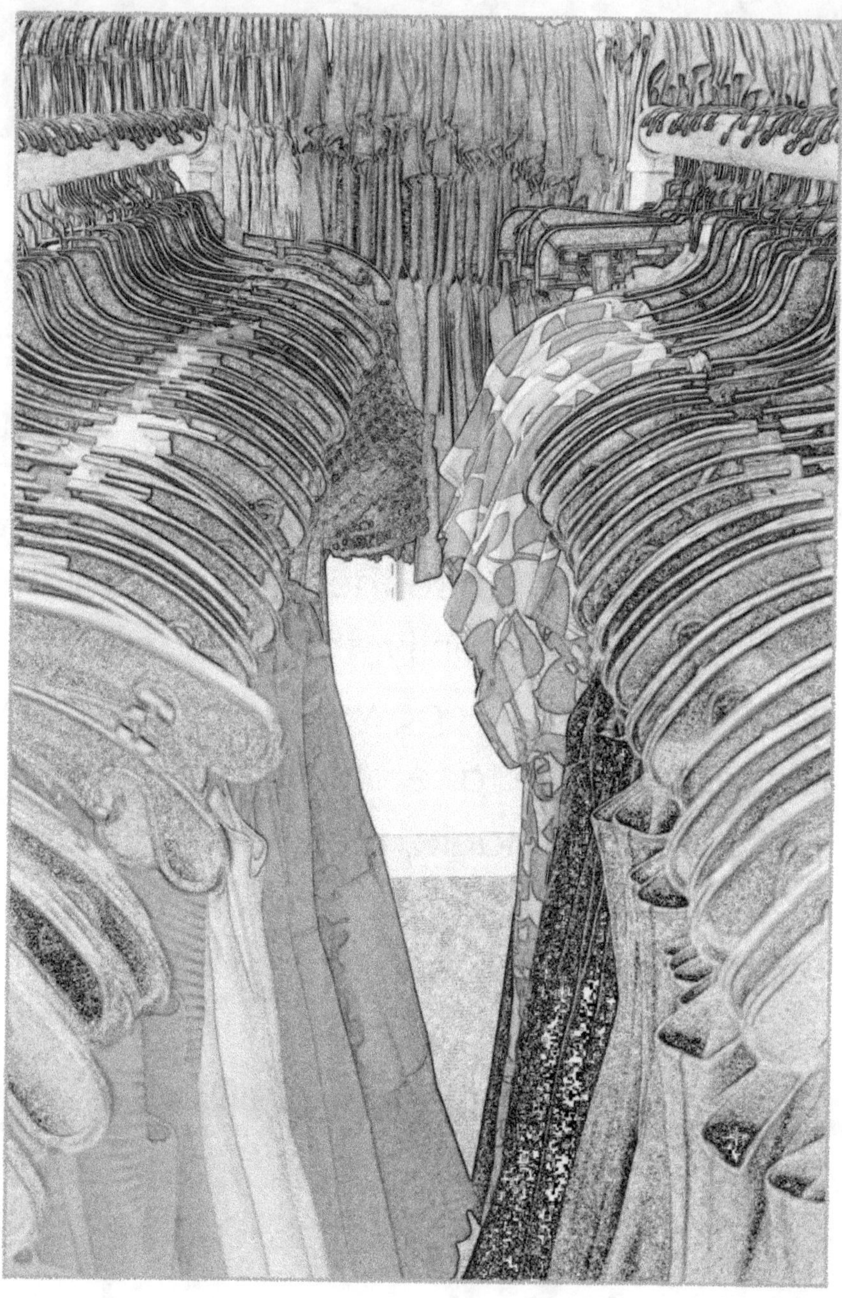

A trip to the opp. shop

"Ready!" cried Olingah Fitzgerald, bounding into the farmhouse kitchen. His cheeks glowed red from the cold Tasmanian winter air. His eyes were bright with excitement. Every other part of his body was covered with woolly winter clothes. His sisters, Leezah and Skye-Maree followed him quickly into the kitchen.

"Well, that must be a new world record!" exclaimed Rommy, their mother. "Are you sure you fed the pigs?" All three nodded vigorously.

"And fed the farm dogs?"

"YUP!"

"And let out the hens?"

"YUP!"

"And fed the pigeons?"

"YUP!!"

"And fed the puppies?"

"YUPP!! We're all done!" cried Olingah as Skye-Maree delivered eight eggs into the basket on the bench. "Let's go!"

Rommy laughed and pointed to the red plastic clock on the wall above the kitchen table. The big hand was pointing to the three and the little hand was just past the seven. Olingah screwed up his nose with concentration. "Big hand on the three. That must be quarter to...quarter past...oh! I don't know...seven, seven, seven like me, half past seven." Olingah pulled off his hat in frustration.

"Good try Olly," said Leezah his eleven-year-old sister. "It's quarter past seven. We still have two hours to wait."

Olingah stomped off to wait impatiently, by himself, in the Ute. But he soon grew very bored and very cold and came back inside.

Two hours finally passed and the family piled into the orange Ute. Flip drove through the open farm gate and turned right, down the long dirt road toward Kellyton. In summer, cars churned up clouds of dust as they passed the farm. But now, the road was wet and muddy.

Flip swung to the left and right avoiding the biggest potholes full of muddy water. Some parts of the road were flooded with a layer of water and fountains of muddy water sprayed up and onto the windows of the car.

"Go faster Daddy!" yelled Skye, loving the water rushing at her face, safe behind the glass.

After twenty minutes of muddy showers and pothole swerving, the Fitzgerald family arrived at the town. They pulled up out the front of a large opp. shop. The gutters were full of dirty water rushing to the drain. Olingah was in such a hurry to get out of the car and into the shop that he stepped right into the water, soaking his shoe, sock and trousers. He thought his mummy would be cross so he quickly stepped out of the water and onto the footpath. He hurried to walk through the shop door before anyone could notice the water slopping from his trousers and shoe.

The bells on the door jangled as Olingah heaved it open. Sue, behind the counter at the end of the shop, looked up with a smile.

"Olly!" she exclaimed, "Did you swim here?" Olingah shook his head vigorously as his family came into the shop.

"Good morning Sue," called Flip. As Rommy came in to the shop she noticed the big puddle of water forming on the mat at Olingah's feet.

"So what is the Fitzgerald family looking for today?" asked Sue.

"Ski clothes!" cried Olingah as he slopped his way to the rack of brightly colored parkas on the left hand wall.

"Mmm, I think we might start with a pair of pants and dry socks Olingah Giachary William."

"Yes Mummy," said Olingah obediently, returning to his mother. Rommy helped him remove his wet clothes. Leezah pulled a pair of second-hand green corduroy overalls from a nearby rack. After he had pulled them on, Olingah went to the table covered in pairs of second hand socks and chose a pair of fluffy red ones. He pushed his cold damp feet into the woolen cocoon. Rommy took his wet shoes, socks and pants and put them in a soggy pile near the door of the shop.

"Thank you Mummy," said Olingah. "Now can we get ski clothes?" Rommy nodded.

Leezah tried on a big green parka that came down to her knees and made her look like a giant green marshmallow. Skye-Maree tried on a purple balaclava that covered everything except her eyes and mouth. She looked like a bank robber. She chased a squealing Olingah around the shop. Flip took some thermal underwear into the change room. A few minutes later he came out wearing woolen rainbow-striped leggings. He paraded in front of his family. Olingah started to giggle.

After about an hour, six green bags were full of ski pants, parkas, beanies, scarves, gloves, thermal underwear, and woolly socks. Sue provided an old plastic bag for the soggy clothes by the front door. Calling goodbye and thank you to Sue, the family walked carefully to the car with their clothes, avoiding the puddles and gutter full of dirty water.

Olingah insisted on wearing his new orange parka on the way home in the car. As the Fitzgeralds drove toward home, he quickly started to feel very hot. He opened the window and let the cold air stream in.

"Olly!" shouted Skye as the wind blew sharply down her neck. "Shut the window!"

"But I'm hot!" moaned Olingah.

"Well take your parka off goose head!" said Skye reaching across her brother to shut the window. Olingah wrestled his sister's arm away from the handle.

"No!"

Skye pressed herself against her brother and leaned toward the handle to wind it. Olingah screeched at Skye and struggled against her.

Flip focused on driving on the wet and muddy road while Rommy turned around from the front seat:

"Olly! Skye-Maree! Is this how you show your gratitude for your new clothes?"

Just as she spoke Skye-Maree lunged across her brother to grab the window handle. But as Olly pushed against her, Skye's hand came down on the door handle. The door of the car swung open. Rommy saw a blur of orange and green tumble from the car as Flip pressed hard on the brakes.

Consideration and courtesy

As the car skidded to a stop, Skye rocked forward until the seat belt jolted her back in her seat. Leezah looked at her mother with wide eyes and an open mouth. Rommy stepped out of the car. She walked carefully to the side of the road. She picked up the Green Bag with Olingah's ski pants from where it had fallen into the mud. Without saying a word she put it into the tray of the Ute, shut the back door of the car, and returned to her seat at the front of the Ute.

Slowly and calmly she turned to face her three stunned children.

"Shall we reflect a little?" she asked, raising her eyebrows high. "What just happened?"

"The bag fell out of the car," said Olingah.

"Mmmm," nodded Rommy.

"Because the door flew open," added Skye.

"Because YOU pulled the door handle," said Olingah glaring at his sister.

"Because YOU bumped me when I was trying to put the window up!" said Skye

"Okay," interrupted Rommy. "Do we all agree that what just happened could have been very dangerous?"

Everyone nodded.

"Olingah what virtue could you have practiced that would have avoided this?"

"I don't know," said Olingah truthfully.

"What about consideration?" suggested Leezah.

"Consideration?" said Olingah softly.

Rommy nodded and turned to Skye. "And you?"

"Um, courtesy?"

Rommy nodded again.

"And because of our lack of consideration and courtesy what did we lose?"

"Unity," said Skye-Maree.

"Safety," said Leezah at the same time.

Rommy nodded and turned back around to face the front.

"Home James," she said to Flip. Flip started the Ute. Olingah slipped out of his new parka, put up the window and locked the door. The dirty water sprayed dramatically against the windows as the children sat silently for the rest of the journey home.

Back at the farmhouse the children were excited to put on the ski clothes they already had, together with the new items they bought at the opp shop. Olingah's ski pants just needed a sponge down from their roll in the mud. When he came into the kitchen where Flip was preparing lunch, Flip covered his eyes with his hand and staggered around pretending to be blind.

"Wow, you are one great big Safety Color son," he said, giving the orange marshmallow man a hug. "We won't lose you on the mountain." Olingah grinned. He couldn't wait to be on the mountain, making a snowman, tobogganing, and learning to ski for the first time. Just one more sleep.

That afternoon the family continued to prepare for their journey to the mountain. Flip and Skye-Maree took the Ute up to the shed. In the shed they found the snow chains which they would need when they got to the icy parts of the mountain road. The chains were covered in dust and spiders' webs. Skye-Maree brushed them down. Flip practiced putting them on the tyres. Then he plunked them in a box on the tray of the Ute.

In the farmhouse Leezah and Rommy cooked a quiche and some sausages which they would take cold the next day. They also made soup which they would take hot in a big thermos. Olingah packed other food into a big box – fruit, crackers, little yoghurts, muesli bars, and best of all, blocks of chocolate. Leezah filled old juice bottles with water and added them to the food box.

Some spare socks, underwear, tracksuit pants, skivvies and jumpers were folded into a carry bag. At the end of the day, if they were cold and wet, it might be good to change into dry clothes for the trip home. And on the very top of the bag were a camera, a purse, and the car keys.

After evening chores, dinner, showers, and prayers, it was time for bed. How badly Leezah,

Skye-Maree, and Olingah wanted the morning to come! How hard they tried to go to sleep quickly! And how difficult it was to calm down with the excitement of the journey to the snow, leaping and dancing around in their minds.

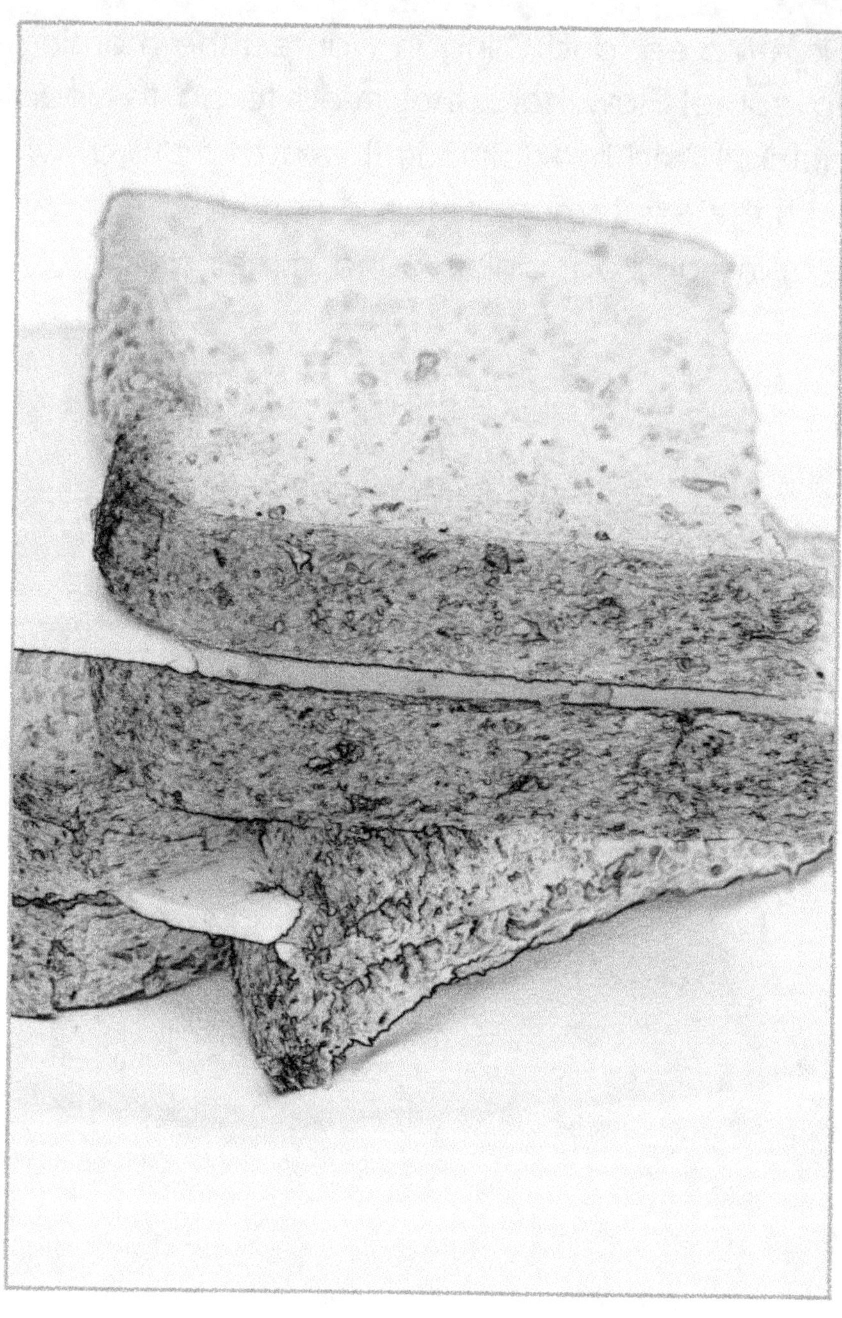

The journey begins

It was very dark and cold outside the farmhouse when Leezah, Skye-Maree, and Olingah climbed out of their beds at five o'clock the next morning. They were very happy to pull on their ski clothes and join their parents in the living room for prayers. Normally they would light the fire in the morning but today the fire was cold in its grate. There was no point in lighting it. The family would be on its way in half an hour.

They read and chanted prayers and Writings. Then, as it was so early and cold, dark and scary, Rommy and Leezah attended to the morning chores in the Ute. They fed the pigs who were barely awake. They drove up the hill from the pigsty to where the farm dogs were tied to their kennels near the shed. They were definitely awake. They were very happy to have an early breakfast. They barked and strained on their chains as Leezah took the bones from the shed fridge. The chickens, who were normally in a rush to get out of the shed, were still nestled on their perches, waiting for sunrise.

While Rommy and Leezah fed the pigeons and puppies behind the farm house, Flip strapped the food box and the clothes bag down on the back of the Ute. He stretched a blue tarpaulin across the tray to protect it from rain. Skye helped him attach the elastic rope to the hooks around the outside wall of the tray. In the cabin of the Ute he put the green bag that held their breakfast.

At ten past six, Rommy turned out the lights and shut the door of the house. She joined the rest of the excited family in the Ute. Their breath made thick clouds in the torchlight as they waited for the car heater to warm up the air. Rommy started the engine of the Ute. Their three-hour journey from Fellowship Farm by the sea, to the top of Ben Lomond, began.

As the car warmed up, many of the layers of clothes were removed. Soon the floor of the Ute had a bright covering of hats, gloves, scarves, jackets and jumpers. Empty tummies started to rumble.

"What's for breakfast Daddy?" asked Leezah from the middle of the back seat.

"Mmm, let's see," said Flip, pulling the bag from the floor to his lap and peering through the early morning darkness. "Looks like dry bread, mouldy cheese, frogs' ears, snakes' bladders and slime. Who's hungry?"

Skye-Maree was already feeling slightly carsick. Her dad's breakfast menu made her feel even worse. She pulled her parka off the floor and leaned her head against the side of the car. She hoped she would fall asleep. Her tummy was starting to swirl in slow gurgling circles.

"Slime please," said Olingah.

"Ah, a very brave boy. A very brave boy," said Flip and handed Olingah a banana and a cheese sandwich.

"Frogs' ears please," said Leezah.

"An excellent choice. An excellent choice," exclaimed Flip and passed Leezah a peanut butter and honey sandwich and an apple.

"Why do you have to say everything twice Dad," moaned Skye.

"Well you may ask! Well you may ask!" replied Flip. "Your question reminds me of a story ...

"In the time of 'Abdu'l-Bahá there was a very dedicated, very wise Bahá'í called Mirza Abu'l Fadl. 'Abdu'l-Bahá loved and trusted him very much. Mirza Abu'l Fadl travelled from Persia to America to teach people about Bahá'u'lláh. He also helped the Bahá'ís learn more about their Faith.

"Sometimes, when he was explaining tricky ideas, he repeated himself. So imagine if he wanted to teach them that six times three is eighteen. He might say 'Six times three is eighteen. So you see, three times six is eighteen. So six lots of three equals eighteen which means that if you have three piles of six oranges you have eighteen oranges. I think you can see now that six times three is eighteen?'

"One day, after one his talks, one of the Bahá'ís walked up to him. Courteously she explained that Americans are very smart. She said, 'You really don't need to repeat yourself so much. If you do, people might get cross with you.'

"Mirza Abu'l Fadl humbly thanked the woman. He explained, 'I was just trying to be clear.' Then he said, 'I just have one question. What was I repeating in my talk?' The woman thought and thought. Then she said, 'Oh I can't remember'. Mirza Abu'l Fadl smiled and said, 'You see Ma'am this is why I repeat myself.'"

The first snow

As the car warmed up, the bellies filled with food, and the story ended, eyelids began to droop. All but Rommy dozed as the family drove along the highway to Launceston and then up the windy bush roads to the foot of the mountain. In the early morning sunlight, Rommy turned off the sealed road onto the dirt road leading up the mountain. The mountain road was rough and bumpy. The children and Flip were bumped and jolted awake. Skye, who usually got very car sick, had managed to avoid it so far by sleeping. As she woke she started to feel queasy.

"Is it okay with everyone if I open my window?" she asked.

"Then we'll be cold," said Olingah.

"I'm feeling really car sick," explained Skye.

"Okay then," said Olingah. "I guess if we get cold we can put our parkas back on."

"Thank for your consideration Olly, and courtesy Skye-Maree," smiled Rommy, looking at them in the rear view mirror.

"Do you want to come sit up the front possum?" asked Flip.

Skye shook her head. She opened her window and leaned her head out. The wind was freezing cold. It took her breath away. She ducked back in gasping. Then she took a big breath and stuck her head out again.

"You can start looking out for snow," said Rommy. All eyes turned to the road and cloud-covered mountain looming above them.

The car wound its way up the mountain. Straining to be the first one to see snow, the children just saw rocks, scraggy bushes and occasional trees. Suddenly Leezah cried:

"SNOW!"

On the side of the road there were small patches of white powder full of sparkling crystals. Olingah wanted to get out and play straight away but his sisters convinced him to be patient and wait until they reached the ski slopes. As they drove higher and higher the snow got thicker. The cloud also got thicker.

Rommy put on the headlights and drove very slowly. As they got closer to the summit other cars came into sight. Some of them had pulled over to the side of the road. Soon Rommy did the same.

"Why are we stopping Mummy?" asked Olingah.

"We need to put the chains on the tyres," answered Flip.

"How come?"

"The chains stop us slipping on the steep and icy parts of the road."

When Flip had put the chains on the wheels Rommy pulled back onto the road.

Leezah looked out the front window of the car. She saw a long narrow road winding with tight corners up Ben Lomond. "That part of the road is called Jacob's Ladder Olly. Its really scary." Rommy slowed the car and headed up Jacob's Ladder. On one side of the road was a steep drop down the mountain. On the other was the mountain itself reaching up to the sky. As Rommy drove carefully round each hairpin bend the children started to sing some prayers.

"Armed with the power of Thy Name, nothing can ever hurt me," they sang in harmony, "and with Thy love in my heart, all the world's afflictions can in no wise alarm me."

Looking down the steep slope of the mountain the children saw an old rusty car that must have fallen off the road some years before and rolled down the rocks. They wondered if anyone had been hurt. As they reached the top of the very windy and steep road, everyone breathed a sigh of relief. They gave Rommy a big clap and cheer. "Thank you for your encouragement and enthusiasm," laughed Rommy.

Soon they pulled into the area where several other cars were parked. The parking lot was covered in dirty snow. At the edge of the car park, where cars and people didn't go, the snow was clean and white. The Fitzgeralds pulled on their boots, jumpers, parkas, scarves, hats and gloves and stepped out of the warm car into freezing cold mountain air. Olingah rushed over to a pile of fresh snow and tried to make a snow ball. The snow did not stick together well and fell through the fingers of his gloves. Turning to Leezah to ask for help, he suddenly realized that his family was already half way up the car park. He ran to join them and followed them up some wooden steps leading to a path.

At the top of the steps the path branched left and right. To the left was a row of wooden buildings. Some were small, and others were two stories high and very large. To the right, the path lead to an office. The path then continued to a large building where visitors to the mountain could buy food, and rent skis and toboggans. And at the very end of the path was a small building with a window from which skiers could buy tickets to use the lifts. The Fitzgeralds turned right. "What are all those houses?" asked Olingah pointing behind them.

"That's where people stay if they are sleeping up here. Some of them belong to families, and some of them are cabins people rent for the night."

"OH! Can we sleep in one of those?!"

"No darling. It's too expensive. We need to drive home tonight," replied Rommy. Olingah knew this was a time to practice gratitude not greediness so he quickly focused on the wonderful opportunity to spend the whole day on the mountain.

He hurried ahead along the path to the place where the Fitzgeralds would rent skis.

Magic Michael the back to front panda

The first thing the children saw when they went through the door was a big hole in the cement floor. It looked like an empty rectangular swimming pool, deeper than Olingah was tall. In the hole was a young man. He was wearing ski overalls and a t-shirt. His face was very brown but he had big white circles around his eyes. Skye thought he looked like a back to front panda. He grinned at the family as they came in and called out "Hullo there! My first customers of the day! You renting skis boots and poles?"

"Poles?" thought Olingah to himself, "Why would we want poles?" But Olingah didn't speak. He was trying to figure out why the man had white patches around his eyes.

"Yes please," said Flip.

Along the side of the hole there were four plastic seats bolted to the ground.

"Take a seat," said the man, "My name is Michael. People call me Magic. I'll be fitting you with your gear today. We'll start with you my lovely," he said smiling at Leezah, "What size is your foot?"

Leezah answered him, and slipped off her red gumboot to reveal a red woolen sock. He reached for a pair of heavy white plastic boots with big clips down the front. Leezah slipped her foot inside. Magic closed the buckles and Leezah nodded to let him know it felt comfortable.

"Now are you a bit of a professional skier?" he asked, with a twinkle in his eye. "Because if you are we'll get you some longer skis."

"Beginner," said Leezah. Magic raised his eyebrows high.

"Oh?" he said and reached for some shorter skis. He attached them to the boots and showed Leezah how to do it herself. Then he measured a couple of ski poles against her body and passed them to her.

"You're all done love. Just carry your skis and poles over there while you wait for the rest of this mob!"

Leezah clumped over to the corner in her heavy ski boots. It was hard to walk and Leezah thought she might fall over and drop her skis and poles, but she made it.

Skye was next. While Magic fitted Skye's boots he chatted and joked and made Skye laugh. She quickly felt very comfortable and so she asked him the question that Olingah had been thinking about.

"Why do you have white patches around your eyes?"

Skye looked at Flip to see if it was okay to ask Magic this question. Flip smiled at Skye and nodded.

"Well, my father was human and my mother was a panda," said Magic with a straight face. Olingah's mouth dropped open. Skye started to giggle. Then Magic explained that during the winter he lived on the mountain. Some days he worked fitting people with rental skis, and many days he skied all day. He explained that the sun reflecting off the snow made his face go brown. Then he pulled some ski-goggles out of his pocket and put them on. The children saw that the white patches were completely covered by the goggles.

"So you see, the sun doesn't get to the skin around my eyes so I end up with white patches."

"Cool!" said Skye turning to Rommy. "Can we rent some goggles?"

Rommy nodded.

When everyone had been fitted with skis, boots, poles and goggles, they stomped outside to the snow. Just outside the building was a large gently sloping area of snow surrounded by a bright yellow plastic fence. In front of the fence was a large sign:

Beginners Ski Lessons

9:30-10:30

10:30-11:30

11:30-12:30

Flip, Rommy, Leezah and Skye-Maree had skied before but it was Olingah's first time. "Perhaps Olly should have a lesson to get him started," suggested Rommy.

"No I want to go up the mountain!" cried Olingah. "I can ski. I don't need a lesson."

"Okay darling," said Rommy. "Let's have a go. Let's put our skis on and head to the hut over there to buy a ticket for the ski lifts."

Everyone put their skis flat on the snow. They put the toe of their boot into the clasp on the ski and pushed down, clipping their skis on, just as Magic had taught them. Rommy and Flip showed the children how to ski up the gentle slope to the hut. Within seconds Olingah and Skye had tumbled onto the snow. They pulled themselves up and kept trying. No sooner had they gone a little way up the slope, than they both started to slide backwards.

"Aaaagh!" cried Olingah as he slid back to where he started and fell over again.

"Keep trying Olly!" called Leezah, turning and sliding forwards down the little slope to help him get up.

Olly and Skye tried to stand back up on their skis, but they kept slipping and falling. In the end they unclipped their boots from their skis, put the skis flat on the snow and stepped back into them. But as soon as they turned the skis up the slope toward the ticket hut, they slid backwards and fell into a pile of snow.

Olly was frowning and frustrated. Skye was laughing at herself and her brother and trying to get him to see the funny side. "How about those lessons?" suggested Flip reaching out a hand to each child and pulling them to their feet.

Olly nodded.

Flip helped Olly slip and slide over to where a few other children were waiting for the 9:30 lesson. Skye eventually made her own way over.

"We'll go buy lift tickets and have some runs, possums," said Flip with a smile, "then we'll meet you back here and take you for a ski, ok?"

Olly and Skye smiled and nodded. The instructors were sliding over to the group now so the children lined up with the others and turned to them. They were wearing black ski pants with a bright green parker. On the back of their parkers was written, in big black letters, INSTRUCTOR. They both had brown faces with white patches around their eyes, just like Magic.

"Hi everyone!" one of the instructors greeted the group loudly, so everyone could hear. "I'm Margaret and this is Steve. We'll be your instructors today." Olly tried to concentrate but he couldn't stop looking at the ring in Margaret's nose and eyebrow. He wondered if it hurt to have your nose and eyebrow pierced.

A long wait

The lesson was so much fun and the hour passed so quickly that when Olly and Skye looked up and saw Flip, Rommy and Leezah behind the fence, they were both surprised and disappointed. Margaret thanked everyone for their great work and high-fived all the children in the group. "Oh, that was so much fun," said Olly sliding over to his family and stopping himself by making a "V" with his skis. "Nice snow plough son," said Flip with a grin.

"Can we have another lesson? Pleeeease?" Flip looked at Rommy. Rommy shrugged her shoulders, nodded and said "Why not?" So Olly and Skye stayed for another hour while Rommy, Flip and Leezah went back up the mountain. Just as the lesson started Olly turned to see them disappearing into the distance, being pulled up the mountain by the poma.

The second lesson was the same as the first one, but with a new group of children. Margaret referred to Olly and Skye as her 'experts' and asked them to demonstrate as she once again taught the basics of skiing. Olly and Skye felt very proud.

Once again the hour passed quickly. As Margaret high-fived the participants at the end, Olly and Skye saw Flip, Rommy and Leezah ski down past the ticket hut to the lesson area. Olly and Skye said, "Thank you very much Margaret" and then skied smoothly over to their family and stopped without falling over.

"Weehooo" cried Leezah as she saw their new skiing ability.

"Well done!" smiled Rommy.

"Can we go on the poma now Mummy?" asked Olingah.

"How about some food first, and then we'll all go out for a ski together?"

Everyone thought food was a great idea.

Outside the building where the family had rented skis there were racks for skis and poles. They unclipped their skis and put them in the racks. Then, feeling like big clomping robots in their ski boots, they stomped inside. As they went in, they took off their hats and mittens and tucked them into their jackets. They hung their jackets on one of the many hooks by the door. They walked past the big hole in the floor where Magic was fitting more people with skis, boots and poles, and into a large room with a wooden floor and lots of tables and benches. The floor was covered in puddles of water where snow had fallen off people's boots and melted.

Three of the tables were occupied. The Fitzgeralds smiled at the other people as they walked past them to a table by the window. The table was covered in a big plastic cover with bright yellow daisies on it. The window looked down the mountain, away from the ski slopes. The land and the sky were white and it was hard to tell where one started and the other finished. In one corner of the room was a microwave so Rommy took the quiche and sausages and put them in the microwave for three minutes. Flip served the soup still hot from the thermos and soon the only sound from the Fitzgerald table was the munching of food. Everyone was ravenously hungry!

After lunch was gobbled up and the containers put away in the bag, the Fitzgeralds headed for the door. As they put their hats, mittens, jackets and goggles back on, Leezah, Skye-Maree and Olingah were bursting with excitement. They wanted to get straight back out to the snow. How they wished they could stay for more than one day! But at least they had the rest of the day to ski. They didn't want to waste one minute! When Olingah and Skye-Maree had their jackets zipped up, Flip gave them each a piece of wire and a green sticker in the shape of a triangle. They threaded the wire through the hole in their zipper and stuck the sticker onto the wire.   This was their lift pass that Rommy and Flip had purchased for them earlier. With that sticker they would be allowed to ride the poma.

Just as the family was heading out the heavy wooden door a tall man and a woman were coming in. They were in matching white and navy blue ski suits, white hats and white ski gloves. Leezah could tell they didn't buy their clothes from the opp. shop! As they passed the children they smiled politely but when they saw Rommy they exclaimed: "Rommy!?"

Rommy looked up and with a big grin said, "Mardi! Bob!" The tall man and the woman hugged Rommy.   Rommy quickly introduced the children, then said, "You remember my husband, Flip?" The couple nodded, as if trying to remember Flip. The adults started talking and the children waited patiently.

When the talking went on and on, the children decided to put on their skis and go up to the poma line to wait there. They whispered to Flip and he nodded. The children were happy to be out on the snow again. Olly and Skye-Maree proudly showed how well they could ski up the gentle slope to the poma. The line was not too long. Many skiers had headed to the cafeteria or their cabins for lunch. By the time the children were at the front of the line their parents were still talking to the couple in the doorway. The children stepped out of the way and let the next person pass. And the next and the next and the next.

"Oh come on Mum!" said Skye, though she knew only Leezah and Olingah could hear her. The children were itching to learn to use the poma and have a ski on the gentle slopes at the front of the mountain. Fifteen minutes passed and the children pulled out of the line and went to slide around on the patch of snow near the poma. The engine of the ski lift was very noisy. The diesel fumes smelt like the tractor on the farm. The children soon grew bored and wished out loud that their parents would Hurry Up!

It felt like hours later when Rommy and Flip finally said goodbye to the couple and skied up to children near the start of the poma.

"Muuum!" said Olingah, "We've been waiting for ages!" Even Leezah was feeling impatient and cross. Rommy and Flip saw the cross faces of their children but they matched them with huge radiant smiles! "Sorry darlings!" said Rommy. "But I think you'll be glad you had to wait a few minutes when you hear what we were talking about with Mardi and Bob."
"What was it?" asked Skye, curious.

"Let's get skiing and we'll talk about it later!" replied Rommy, and headed for the line. Impatience was forgotten as the Fitzgerald family followed Rommy to the poma line. The line was very short now so they only had to wait a moment before it was their turn to ride the poma.

A crash

Running from the bottom of the mountain to half way up the front slope was a long wire held up by metal pillars, like telegraph poles. All along the wire, a few meters apart there were long plastic poles hanging down almost to the ground. On the bottom of each pole was a little circle of plastic. Olly watched as the person before him put the pole between his legs and rested his bottom on the plastic circle. Then he saw that as the wire moved it pulled the plastic pole forward and the person skied along, going up the mountain. It looked very easy.

Olly stood in place and waited for the poma to come around the corner. The pomas going up the mountain were pulling people, but once the people got off up the top of the mountain, the pomas came down empty. As the next one swung around the corner and came toward Olly he reached out and tried to grab it. But when he tried to put it between his legs he lost his balance. Olly fell over and the poma went springing forward and up the mountain.

"Woops!" said Olly and got up again. He reached for the next one, got it between his legs but his skis were facing off to the left, so when the poma pulled him forward he tipped over. Once again the poma went springing forward and on up the mountain.

Flip slid forward and helped Olly to his feet. "Good opportunity to practice determination eh Ollyboy?" and Olly nodded.

He stood with his skis facing straight forward. Flip grabbed the poma and put it between Olly's legs so his bottom was resting on the round disc.

"Hold on tight son," called Flip as Olly was pulled forward, first jerkily, then more smoothly up the mountain.

The rest of the family caught the pomas after Olly and soon they were all halfway up the mountain on a flat piece of snow. Over to the side and above where they stood they could see steeper slopes. Experienced skiers flew down the slopes, even jumping over small cliffs.

"Wow! Look at that!" said Skye-Maree pointing to a girl skiing quickly down the top of the mountain which seemed to go straight down without even a slope!

Then they turned to the gentle slop below them, leading down to the start of the poma and to the ticket hut. The children felt a surge of excitement.

"Ready?" called Rommy. Four brightly colored woolen hats nodded yes. Rommy pushed off gently and began to cut across the front of the mountain doing a snow plough. When she had crossed the slope she turned and came slowly back the other way, snaking her way down the mountain. Leezah went next. She copied Rommy. Then it was Olly's turn. The slope was a little steeper than it looked and Olly found himself rushing a little faster than he expected but he loved it. He successfully maneuvered his first turn and was crossing back over the slope when he heard a loud "Eeeeeeeeeeee". Skye-Maree had pushed off too hard and was charging down the mountain. Instead of big slow curves, Skye was rushing almost straight down.

Skye started to panic and her mind went blank. She could hear that her family was yelling advice but it was all just a blur of sound. She could see people skiing on the slope below her and wondered if she would crash into them. For a second Skye-Maree wondered if she was about to die. Suddenly she cried out "Ya Baha'u'l-Abha" and as she said the prayer she sat down hard on the snow. One ski flew off and she spun around onto her back. Her body slid for a few meters down the mountain and then stopped. The ski that had come off went sliding off down the slope, stopping way below where people were lined up to ride the poma.

Skye looked up into the white sky. She felt bruised and sore on her bottom and on the back of her head. Within a few seconds Flip and Rommy were at her side. After some time they helped her to slowly sit up. "You okay possum?" Flip asked. A couple of tears trickled down Skye's cheeks. "Yup," she nodded slowly.

"Nothing broken?" asked Rommy. Skye started to unclip the remaining ski and slowly push herself up to a stand. She shook her head in answer to Rommy's question.

As she gently dusted herself off, Olingah and Leezah skied over.

"You okay sister?" asked Leezah.

"Look at your ski! It's already in the line up for the poma!"

Skye looked at Rommy. "How am I going to get down the mountain on one ski?"

"You wait here," replied Rommy. "I'll bring it to you."
Rommy went sliding off down the mountain making occasional turns with perfect control. When she reached the bottom of the slope, she picked up Skye's ski and put it under her arm. A few minutes later she was sliding past the family on her way back up the mountain. The children waved as she slid past.

Soon after she slid past, being pulled by the poma, Rommy appeared on the slope and slid quickly down towards them. She turned just as she reached them, sending a little spray of snow onto Flip's legs.

"Eh! Watchit!" Flip raised his eyebrows and bared his teeth at Rommy.

Skye took the ski from Rommy and attached it to her boot.

"Ready to get back on the horse Skye?" asked Rommy with a wink. Skye nodded.

Slowly she pushed off and, together with the rest of her family, wound her way carefully down the slope with her skis in the shape of a big V.

Exciting news

The rest of the afternoon was full of riding pomas, falling off pomas, getting up, falling down, tears, laughter, bruises, determination, exhilaration, courage, fear, victory, encouragement, and fun. At 4:30 they lined up for their last ride up the mountain as the poma was going to stop running after that. By their last run down the mountain, all the children felt confident and comfortable. They raced each other to the bottom. Rommy and Flip raced down after them and pulled to a stop with a spray of snow across the children.

"Time to take our skis back," smiled Rommy.

Leezah, Skye and Olingah's hearts were full of gratitude for the wonderful day of skiing. They were also full of longing, wishing they didn't have to leave.

"Thank you for a wonderful day," said Leezah.

"Yes thank you!" said Skye and Olingah.

"You're welcome possums," said Flip. "We honor your gratitude."

The family skied slowly down past the ticket hut until they arrived at the building where they had rented their skis and eaten their lunch. They unclipped their skis and carried them in. It felt strange to be clomping clumsily instead of gliding freely. Inside, the cafeteria smelt of hot chocolate and hot meat pies. The children's tummies rumbled loudly.

They walked over to the big hole in the ground. Magic smiled up at them. "So how did you go?"

"GREAT!" said Olingah. "When I'm old like you I am going to get a job here too! "I want to ski every day all day!"

"Good one!" grinned Magic, taking their skis, boots and poles, one by one.

Their socks were wet with sweat and melted snow so they flopped over to the tables and sat down to change into dry socks before they put their gumboots back on. Their mittens and hats and skivvies were also damp with sweat.

As they put on their gumboots Olly looked out the window. The sun had set and darkness was falling over the mountain.

"Oh I wish we could stay for another day," he said without thinking and then quickly put his hand over his mouth. Olingah knew that he should be grateful not greedy. "Oh! It just popped out," he said. "Thank you for a lovely day Mummy! Thank you Daddy!"

"You're welcome darling. Now, would you like to know what we were talking about with Mardi and Bob?" The children nodded. Rommy explained that Mardi and Bob were friends of her parents who lived in Hobart. Mardi and Bob owned one of the cabins on the mountain. In fact they had owned it for more than twenty years and used to bring their children here when they still lived at home. Now the children were grown there were a couple of spare bedrooms in the cabin. Mardi and Bob had invited the Fitzgerald family to stay with them in their cabin. Six little eyes opened wide and three little mouths dropped open.

"So we said, no thanks. Our children would like to get back to the farm tonight," said Flip.

"DAAAD!!" said Leezah. But she knew her dad was joking.

"So are we really going to sleep in the cabin in the snow tonight?" said Olingah jumping up in his dry socks and landing in a big puddle of water.

Rommy nodded, "Would you like to?" She was suddenly swamped by hugging arms and grinning faces.

Struggling under the sea of arms Rommy continued: "We won't be able to rent skis tomorrow as we can only afford that for one day."

"But we could build a snow-woman!" exclaimed Skye.

"Yes! And we can hire toboggans," added Rommy.

The children thought they would burst from excitement. They talked over the top of each other, sharing ideas and plans for the night and day ahead.

Just then, Mardi appeared in the doorway of the dining room. "Hi Rommy," she said and smiled at everyone else. "Bob's got the pasta cooking. If anyone's hungry you're welcome to come on over now."

Everyone quickly finished putting their socks and boots on. They pushed their arms back into the parkas, which now felt cold and soggy. "Yuck!" said Skye-Maree.

Feeling rather uncomfortable in their cold wet ski gear the Fitzgeralds followed Mardi down the path and up the other side to the cabins. The path was lit by some lamp posts. The snow in the lamp light shone like crystal. The path took them over a small wooden bridge. Under the bridge was a stream. In the lamp light, the children could see that whole sections of the stream were frozen solid. They looked forward to having a play there tomorrow.

When they arrived at the cabin, the smell of pasta and pesto filled their nostrils. Everyone took their boots off outside and carried them in. Mardi showed them a little room near the front door which was extra warm and dry. She showed them where to hang their parkas, hats, mittens, socks and boots and explained that this was the drying room. "By tomorrow morning, your clothes will be dry and warm again," she explained. "When you've had your shower you can bring your ski pants and hang them here too."

Leezah was the first in the shower. The warm water rushing over her cold, damp, bruised and tired body felt delicious. All her muscles were aching. Some of them she had rarely used before! She felt she could stay in the warm waterfall all night. But she knew others were waiting, so she quickly washed and stepped out. On the wooden floor was a fluffy mat and warm air was blowing from a vent in the corner of the room. Leezah toweled herself down with the big green towel Mardi had given her. She then pulled on the spare clothes they had brought to change into for the drive home. Olly, Skye, Flip and then Rommy also quickly washed and dressed. Leezah hung her wet ski pants in the drying room.

She came into the living room, which was connected to the kitchen where Bob and Mardi were preparing dinner. "Can I help?" she asked.

"Yesh," replied Mardi through a mouthful of carrot. She showed Leezah the drawer with place mats and napkins and indicated for Leezah to set the table.

One by one the rest of the Fitzgeralds hung their wet ski pants and came into the living room. Two walls were made of windows looking down and across the mountain away from the ski slopes. It was completely dark now so Bob pulled the wooden shutters and shut the curtains to keep in the heat. When Rommy joined them, Bob said, "Let's eat!" There were no arguments.

The wooden table was set for seven. There were not quite enough chairs so one place had a metal garbage bin with a cushion on top of it instead of a chair. "I would offer to sit on the bin," said Bob, "but I would probably squash it flat like an old coke can. So Olingah, would you mind sitting on that? You look like the lightest." Olingah was very happy to sit on the bin, so long as he didn't fall in. In the middle of the table was a bowl full of salad and a big steaming pot of pasta. The children felt like they had never been so hungry in all their lives!

Who's Who?

After two big bowls of pasta and salad, and a bowl of ice cream, all tummies were very full. "Why don't you go have a look in the bedroom cupboards," suggested Bob. "Our children had a lot of board games which we still haven't given away. You might find something fun to play." The children cleared the table and thanked Bob and Mardi for a delicious dinner. They were very happy to explore the cupboards. As they opened the bedroom door they heard Mardi remark to Flip and Rommy that they were "delightful children". Rommy started to talk about spiritual education, and soon the adults were deep in conversation.

In the bedroom the children found shelves full of games. There was Chinese Checkers, Monopoly, The Game of Life, an old dart board and some darts, UNO cards, Who's Who?, and lots of other games. They decided to play 'Who's Who?' Skye-Maree went first. She picked a card with a face on it. The face had black skin, brown eyes, long hair, a beard, moustache, and a hat. Leezah opened her tray with rows of different faces and started to ask questions.

"Is it female?"

"No." Leezah pushed down half of her faces.

"Does it have a moustache?"

"Yes." Leezah pushed down another eight faces.

Leezah kept asking questions until the only face left standing on her tray had black skin, brown eyes, long hair, a beard, moustache and a hat. She showed Skye.

"Correct!"

Olingah's turn was next but when the girls finished their game they noticed that Olingah was curled up like a little wombat on the floor near the bed, fast asleep.

They lifted him into one of the beds that Mardi and Bob had prepared for the children.

Leezah and Skye sat on the edge of Olingah's bed and sang him some prayers while he slept.

From the living room the girls could hear the sounds of Flip telling one of his funny stories and the others laughing. They put away the games and climbed into the other beds. It was still very early, but after their early start and very busy active day, the girls were already starting to feel sleepy. As they lay in their beds Leezah said to Skye: "Let's play High-Low."

"What's High-Low?" asked Skye-Maree.

Leezah explained that at school every Monday morning her class played High-Low. Each student had a chance to say what was the highlight of their weekend and what was the lowlight. What was best and what was worst. Through this game Leezah had lots of opportunities to talk about the Bahá'í Faith to her teacher and classmates. Often Leezah's highlight of the weekend   was a Holy Day, 19-Day feast, Ayyam-i-Ha, or a children's class.

"Okay," said Skye-Maree. "You go first."

"Um, my High was … EVERYTHING! Having breakfast in the car, skiing all day long, getting to sleep on the mountain! My Low was …your accident at the start of the day."

"Same," said Skye. "My high was everything. Even my accident. You know as soon as I said

Ya-Baha'u'l-Abha I knew what I had to do – just sit down. So even that was a good experience. My Low was having to put my soggy cold parka, mittens, and hat back on to walk to the cabin!"

Skye-Maree let out a big yawn. And Leezah followed. They pulled the curtains back from the window and looked out. There were no stars to be seen. The night sky was dark and cloudy. As Leezah drifted off to sleep she wondered if it might snow tomorrow.

By the time Flip and Rommy had finished their conversation, washed the dishes and came to say goodnight to their children, Leezah, Skye and Olingah were fast asleep. As always Skye had kicked her blanket onto the floor and Olingah was burrowed down under his. They were all dreaming of flying down the mountain on super fast skis.

Dawn and the Snow-woman

The children stirred early and for a few minutes they could not work out where they were. There were no familiar sights, sounds, or smells. The bedroom felt unusually warm and everything was silent. Slowly they fully woke up and remembered the wonderful adventure of the day before and the promise of more that day. They had a quick whispered consultation and then quietly padded out to the drying room. As Mardi had promised, their soggy ski clothes from the day before were dry and warm. They took them back into the bedroom and turned on the light. They took off the clothes they had worn to bed and pulled on the ski clothes. When they were dressed they tiptoed to the front door of the cabin. They quietly opened the cabin door and before stepping out, they put on their gumboots.

Outside it was still dark. The lamps shone on the path in front of the cabins but the rest of the mountain was hidden in the darkness. "Look!" Skye pointed. In the light of the lamps, the children could see little flakes of snow falling gently to the ground.

"It's snowing!" exclaimed Olingah in a loud whisper.

The children bent over to gather the newly fallen snow into a ball. The snow stuck together well when they pressed it firmly.

"Let's make a snow-woman!" Skye suggested. Olingah and Leezah agreed.

In the lamplight the children rolled and pressed the snow on the path until they had three small balls to use as a base, middle and head for their snow-woman.

They were just putting the balls on top of each other when the cabin door opened and Rommy stuck her head out.

"Mmm, I thought I might find the escapees here!" she said to Flip who was standing behind her.

"Look Mummy," called Olly gently. "It's snowing! And we're making a snow-woman!"

"Beautiful darling! Mardi and Bob are still sleeping so keep playing quietly. When they wake up we'll have some breakfast."

As the children worked on their snow-woman they noticed that lights were starting to come on in the cabins all along the path. The balls of snow were firmly balanced on each other. It was time to look for eyes, a nose, arms and buttons for their snow-woman. The sun was just beginning to rise, which made it easier to find some twigs and stones to stick into the snow. Leezah had just put two stones from the creek at the bottom of the biggest ball, to make feet, when the cabin door opened.

"Come and look at what we made Dad," called Olingah.

Flip came outside in his bare feet, hopping from one to the other on the cold snow. "Very creative!" said Flip making steamy puffs with every breath. "Now, how about some breakfast possums?" Flip turned and hip hopped back into the cabin. The children admired their work and then followed their bouncing father.

Inside the cabin, Mardi and Rommy were cooking some porridge and making toast. During the winter, Mardi and Bob stayed at the cabin on the mountain for weeks at a time. They would go to Launceston about once a week to get groceries, so they only had very limited supplies of fruit and fresh vegetables. But they had plenty of food that could easily be stored or frozen, like pasta, porridge and bread, and were happy to share.

As the children sat up at the table Rommy served them each a big bowl of steaming porridge. The children added a big dollop of honey each and poured lots of milk on top. The milk helped to cool the porridge down. Even so, in her rush, Skye-Maree burnt her tongue on the hot mush. She could hardly taste the honey or the creamy milk after that.

After her porridge Leezah ate two pieces of toast with vegemite. She really wanted another piece but she worried that Mardi and Bob might think she was greedy. But when Olingah got full half way through his second piece of toast Leezah was quick to offer to help out. When they had finished the children cleared the table and washed the dishes.

"After prayers, can we go out in the snow?" asked Skye, wrapping her arms around her mother who was still sitting at the table with Flip, Mardi and Bob.

"Yes we will."

Skye turned to Mardi and Bob and said "We always have prayers in the morning. Would you like to join us for some prayers?"

Bob looked a bit surprised but Mardi said, "We'd love to. What do you do?"

"Well we normally have prayer books and the guitar, but we didn't bring them up the mountain because we didn't plan to stay the night. So, we could just sit around the table and sing some prayers."

"That sounds great," said Mardi. "It might do us good Bob!"

Bob looked doubtful. He asked Skye, "Why do you pray Skye?"

Skye explained that there are two reasons they pray: "First of all, because we love God. Just like you love Mardi, so you want to talk to her and listen to her. And because we love God we want to talk to God and listen to God. And also, because prayer is like food for our soul. We have porridge for our bodies and prayers for our soul."

Bob looked very impressed. "Well, let's have some soul porridge then!" he laughed. The children nodded and sat themselves back down at the table.

"O my God! O my God! Unite the hearts of thy servants and reveal to them Thy great purpose," Rommy started to sing and the rest of the family joined in.

The Fitzgeralds sang many prayers while Mardi and Bob listened. After they had finished the children went off to brush their teeth and gather their belongings together. When they were ready to go, they came back to the living room. Mardi and Bob had given the family some peanut butter sandwiches and filled the thermos with hot chocolate for lunch. The Fitzgeralds still had some food left over from the day before as well so they knew they would have plenty to eat. The Fitzgeralds thanked Mardi and Bob very much for inviting them to stay. They slipped their feet into their gumboots. As they left the cabin they walked past their little snow-woman and admired her. The family headed towards the building where they had rented skis and had lunch the day before. This was where they would hire their toboggans. This was where their new

adventure would begin. But that, is another
story.

BOOK TWELVE

THE SNOWY SUPER-GLIDER-SLIP-N-SLIDER

The Fitzgerald children continue their adventures in the snow in this, the twelfth book about the family on Fellowship Farm. They have opportunity to try tobogganing. They also make some new friends who teach them about courage. After the snow comes some delicious hot chocolate and homemade fudge that mysteriously makes Olingah cry. The journey home from the snow is not without event as the family has opportunity to help a baby whose mother has been in an unfortunate accident.

Choosing toboggans

Magic was in the cement hole, fitting a family with boots and skis when the Fitzgerald Family entered the building. They waved hello as they walked past. He winked back. Around the corner from Magic's pit was a wooden wall with about twenty big nails hammered all the way along. From the nails hung toboggans. Some were yellow. Some were orange and a few were a faded red. They were made of hard plastic and each one had a rope attached to the front that formed a handle. Olingah jumped up and down. "Look Mum! Look! Here they are! Can I have a yellow one? Please? Wow! There are so many! Look at that red one – it's like a double decker toboggan! Look how big it is! Which one do you want Skye-Maree? I like the yellow one!"

"I honor your enthusiasm Olly," laughed Rommy, "but how about some peacefulness as we make our decisions?" Leezah went to the checkout and asked how much it cost to rent a toboggan for the day. There were two options – they could rent them for half a day up to 12 noon or for the full day up to 4:30pm. Rommy and Flip consulted. Olly tried to stand still but his excitement was bubbling out. Finally Flip said: " So, we need to decide what we want to do. We can rent four toboggans for half a day, or we can rent two toboggans for the whole day." Then it was the children's turn to consult.

"Let's get four for half a day," suggested Leezah.

"But then we'll have to go home at lunchtime!" said Olingah. Olingah's face started to crumple into a frown.

"If we have four toboggans we can all ride together instead of taking it in turns," said Skye-Maree.

"And, if we toboggan in the morning, all together, then we can make a snowman or a snow cave in the afternoon," said Leezah.

"Good idea!" exclaimed Olingah. "Let's do that!"

Olly chose a yellow toboggan. Leezah and Skye-Maree chose orange. Rommy and Flip rented the double decker red one. The toboggans were bigger and heavier than they looked hanging on the wall. Luckily the children didn't have to carry them far. As soon as they got outside they put the toboggans on the ground and pulled them by the rope over the snow. Rommy and Flip led them down hill away from the ski slopes. They found a long hill of snow that had no trees or rocks in the middle. At the bottom, the slope flattened out a bit so they had a good place to slow down and stop. If they didn't stop there they would have a steep, fast and rocky ride down the next part of the mountain!

The hill was covered in a thin layer of newly fallen snow. Everyone was eager to start tobogganing. They lined up the four toboggans at the top of the hill. As they climbed on, Flip warned: "It might be harder than you think to stay balanced so don't leave your patience and determination at the top of the hill!" Flip turned to Rommy and with a low bow and sweep of his arm toward the toboggan said: "Milady", inviting her to get onto the toboggan. Rommy climbed on to the front and took hold of the rope. Flip climbed on behind her and wrapped his arms around her waist. He looked across at Olly, Skye and

Leezah. Eyes were bright. Cheeks red. Grins wide.

Leezah called: "Ready! Set! Go!" They pushed off and started to slide. As they gathered speed Olly and Skye-Maree wobbled, shrieked and squealed. At the steepest part of the hill they rushed over the snow. It felt like they were flying! Their ears were full of wind and tears streamed from their eyes. They clung tightly to their ropes as their hearts raced.

It was hard to steer the toboggans. They seemed to just follow their own path. After hitting a small bump in the snow Leezah's toboggan started to veer to the right toward Skye-Maree's. "LEEZAH!!" screamed Skye-Maree. But just in time Skye-Maree whizzed on down the mountain. Leezah kept veering right and crossed over the tracks Skye-Maree had made. She tried to correct her path by leaning to the left. But she leaned too far to the left. The toboggan tipped. Suddenly Leezah was sprawled across the snow, sliding down the hill, clinging to the rope of her toboggan and having some very cold morning tea!

The Abominable Snowman

When Leezah stopped sliding, her face and hat and snow suit were covered in snow. She could feel the icy clumps on her eyebrows and in her ears. She lifted her head and saw her family at the bottom of the hill. She waved her hand and started to giggle. She pulled herself onto her toboggan, lying on her tummy, and pushed off with her toes against the snow. She slithered her way to the bottom of the hill. When Skye-Maree and Olingah saw that she was covered in snow, and that she was giggling, they also started to giggle.

Skye-Maree pulled her toboggan away from her sister and cried: "It's the Abominable Snowman!"

"Yeah! The anominabal snowman!" cried Olingah and scrambled up the side of the slope, dragging his toboggan and laughing.

Leezah followed after them, struggling to run up hill in the snow in her gumboots, but going as fast as she could. She caught up with her sister, tipped her on the arm and said: "Now you're the 'anominabal' snowman," and moved away as fast as she could.

Skye-Maree was the strongest of the three children. She was tall for her age with long strong legs and she was very fit. She pushed hard against the slippery snow and chased her siblings up the slope. Playing tip all the way up the hill they arrived at the top, hot and panting. Rommy and Flip made their way much more slowly. When they arrived at the top, the children were all lined up and ready to go again. "You go," smiled Rommy. "Don't wait for us!"

"Ok!" said Olingah. "Ready! Set! Go!" and off they flew, over the mound and down the front of the hill. Rommy and Flip watched as the bright colors of toboggans and ski suits, hats and mittens zoomed away. They watched as it all ended in a jumbled mess at the bottom of the hill where all three toboggans slid into each other and overturned.

As the children scrambled up the hill for the second time they saw another family arriving at the hilltop. The family had a rented toboggan too. It was a double decker red one. "Look!" called Skye-Maree who was ahead of Leezah and Olingah, "Some more children to play with!" They hurried up the hill to meet them.

They saw two girls and two adults. Rommy and Flip were already introducing themselves and starting to chat. One girl was about Olingah's age, seven years. The other was about Leezah's age, eleven. They noticed that the younger girl walked a bit behind her sister, with her hand on her shoulder. "Hullo," panted Skye-Maree as she reached the top. "My name is Skye, and that's my brother Olly and sister Leezah," she said pointing behind her. The girls smiled shyly.

"Hi!" said Olly as he reached the top of the hill and threw himself onto the ground, puffing and panting. "Want to have a race down the hill with us?"

The girls nodded.

Rommy and Flip stayed up the top of the hill talking to the parents of the girls. The older sister – whose name was Laurel – lead the younger girl to the top of the hill and held the toboggan. Her sister - Tahlia – climbed in. Laurel sat behind Tahlia, with her legs wrapped around her and they both held the rope. When the Fitzgerald children were lined up, they said to Laurel: "You can say ready set go."

Laurel was already starting to feel comfortable with the friendly children and her shyness was evaporating. She smiled and called out: "Ready! Set! Go!"

Everyone pushed off and raced down the hill. Laurel and Tahlia were first to the bottom by far. And it was then that the Fitzgerald children learned something very surprising.

A courageous friend

"You hold the toboggan Tahlia," said Laurel as they climbed off at the bottom of the hill. With one hand Tahlia held the rope of the toboggan, which trailed behind her. Then Tahlia reached out her other hand and Laurel guided it to her shoulder. Laurel walked ahead and Tahlia followed closely behind, her hand never leaving her sister's shoulder.

"Why are you walking in a chain?" asked Olly. "Does it make it easier to pull the toboggan?"

"No," said Laurel. "We walk like this because Tahlia is blind."

Olly's mouth dropped open. He looked at his sisters. "So do you mean when you went whizzing down that hill you couldn't see where you were going, Tahlia?"

Tahlia nodded.

"Wow! That is sooo courageous! Isn't it scary?"

Tahlia nodded again, and smiled, "But tobogganing is fun!"

The children trudged up the hill, dragging their toboggans in silence but Olly's mind was racing. At the top of the hill he announced a challenge for everyone.

"This time when we go down the hill, let's all keep our eyes shut!"

"Yes," exclaimed Skye-Maree. "Let's pull our scarves and hats over our eyes so we can't cheat."

The children lined up at the top of the hill, then pulled their scarves up and hats down. Laurel described what they were doing so Tahlia understood and Tahlia smiled. They looked like a row of bandits about to rob a bank. A shiver went down Leezah's spine and she wondered if she would be able to keep her eyes covered all the way down.

Laurel called out: "Ready, Set, Go!"

With much less gusto than usual the Fitzgerald children pushed off and started to slither down the hill. With their eyes covered it was harder to balance. Their toboggans slid faster and faster. They started to veer to the right and to the left. They wondered if they would ever stop. Their chests felt tight. Their hearts raced. Just as they started to feel overwhelmed with panic their toboggans collided, overturned and they sprawled across the snow, slipping and sliding like brightly colored blind seals on the mountain side.

They scrambled to free their eyes from their covers and crouched, panting, and relieved in the snow. "That was terrifying!" exclaimed Skye-Maree. Her siblings nodded their agreement. Slowly, with their eyes wide open, they slithered down the slope to where Laurel and Tahlia were waiting patiently for them.

"How was it?" asked Laurel.

"Scar-eee!" replied Olingah. "I really honor your courage Tahlia!"

When they got to the top of the hill again they could hear Rommy talking with Laurel and Tahlia's parents. "So, you see we must be lovers of the Light," she explained, "and not attached to any particular lamp from which the Light has shone." The children continued to race down the hill and stagger up it for many hours. By noon they were very hungry and thirsty and their parents were getting very cold.

The snow started to fall again, making it impossible to see the top of the hill from the bottom of the hill. The families decided to go to the hut for lunch.

It was very hard to find the energy to pull the toboggans up the hill to the hut. Finally, soggy, hot, sweaty and with aching legs, they arrived at the hut. They tapped the extra snow from their boots and went inside. The air inside was warm and dry. Like yesterday, it smelt of hot chocolate and meat pies. They dragged their toboggans over to the wall and left them on the floor under the nails. Then they peeled off their soggy hats, gloves, scarves, jackets, boots, and socks, and made a big wet pile on one of the free tables in the cafeteria.

Flip brought everyone jugs of water and cups, then went back for nine big mugs of hot chocolate with marshmallows floating on top. Rommy, and Tahlia's parents laid out the food to share lunch. Nine very hungry people feasted on peanut butter sandwiches, apples, bananas, yoghurt, chicken drumsticks, potato salad, humus and crackers, nuts and sultanas. When every last crumb had been eaten, Tahlia's father pulled out the best of all. They had a big box of homemade chocolate fudge.

"My grandma's fudge is the BEST!" grinned Tahlia as she heard the lid being removed from the plastic box. Olingah, Skye-Maree and Lizah were very happy to find out if Tahlia was right.

There was enough for each child to have a long finger of fudge. Laurel passed the box around so that each child could take one. She offered it first to Skye-Maree. Normally Rommy and Flip didn't let them eat sweets. Skye-Maree looked at her parents, eyes wide, wondering if they would agree. They looked back at her, matching her wide eyes. Then they nodded. Skye-Maree reached out and took a finger of fudge. Olly was sitting on his hands so that he wouldn't be rude and grab a piece. When he was offered the fudge his hands flew out from under his legs and gratefully seized the fudge. Leezah also took a piece. They licked and nibbled their fudge. They wanted it to last as long as possible.

Even though Olingah loved the sweet creamy taste in his mouth, as he ate it he started to feel sadder and sadder. By the time he had finished his fudge, little tears were trickling down his face. Skye-Maree noticed the tears. "Are you sad because your fudge is all finished?" she asked kindly. Olly shook his head. The tears trickled off his chin onto the sticky fingers he was licking. "What's the matter Olly?" asked Rommy. The tears started to flow even faster. It was very hard for Olly to speak. Finally he said, quietly to his mother, "Don't you love me any more Mummy?"

Eating rubbish

Rommy was very surprised to hear Olingah's question.

"Of course I love you very much Olly." Rommy's face was very puzzled. She looked at Flip, but his eyes were wide and he shrugged his shoulders and lifted his hands as if to say, "I have no idea what's going on!" Everyone around the table sat still, wondering why Olingah was upset. "Why did you ask me if I love you?" Rommy said softly to her son.

Olingah's nose was running now and his tears were flowing. Leezah passed him a napkin to wipe his face. When he had blown his nose he said: "Whenever we ask if we can have sweets you always say no. Whenever we ask why, you always say you love us too much to let us put rubbish in our bodies. But today you let us have a whole slice of fudge. So does that mean you don't love us as much any more?"

Rommy looked very relieved. Leezah tried not to laugh but a little giggle squeaked out.

Through wet lashes Olingah scowled at his sister. The squeaking stopped.

"No, Olingah. I still love you just as much as always. And it's true that it's not good to put lots of sugar in our bodies. But we can also occasionally have treats so long as we practice the virtue of moderation."

Now it was Olingah's turn to look relieved. "What's moderation?" he asked.

Flip said, "Let me tell you a story about 'Abdul-Bahá and moderation." Olly nodded enthusiastically. "Two stories actually," added Flip. "The first is one you know I think, about 'Abdu'l-Baha's journey on a coach to Haifa:

"One day 'Abdu'l-Bahá wanted to go from Akka to Haifa. He went to take an inexpensive seat in a regular coach. The driver was surprised and must have asked himself why 'Abdu'l-Bahá was so frugal as to ride in this cheap coach. "Surely, Your Excellency would prefer to travel in a private carriage," he exclaimed. "No," replied the Master, and He traveled in the crowded coach all the way to Haifa. As He stepped down from the coach in Haifa a distressed fisherwoman came to Him and asked for His help. All day she had caught nothing and now had to return to her hungry family. 'Abdu'l-Bahá gave her a good sum of money, turned to the driver and said, "Why should I ride in luxury while so many are starving?"[1]

"Yes, I know that story from children's classes," said Olly.

"Very very good," nodded Flip. "So you know this was the sort of decision that 'Abdu'l-Bahá usually made?" Olingah nodded.

"But!" exclaimed Flip dramatically throwing his arms into the air and rocking back on the bench, "one day, during 'Abdu'l-Bahá's travels the friends booked Him into a very modest hotel. Then 'Abdu'l-Bahá surprised them by saying that on that night they were all going to stay in a very lovely, and more expensive place. Maybe He wanted the friends to understand moderation. Moderation means not going to extremes."

Olly still looked confused. Leezah explained her understanding.

---

[1] Story from Ruhi Book 3: Teaching Children's Classes, Grade 1; pp. 43-44

"We should fill our bodies with healthy food nearly all the time but it's okay to have one little sweet every now and then."

Olly nodded. He noticed there were some pieces of fudge left in the box.

"What about two little sweets every now and then?" he asked.

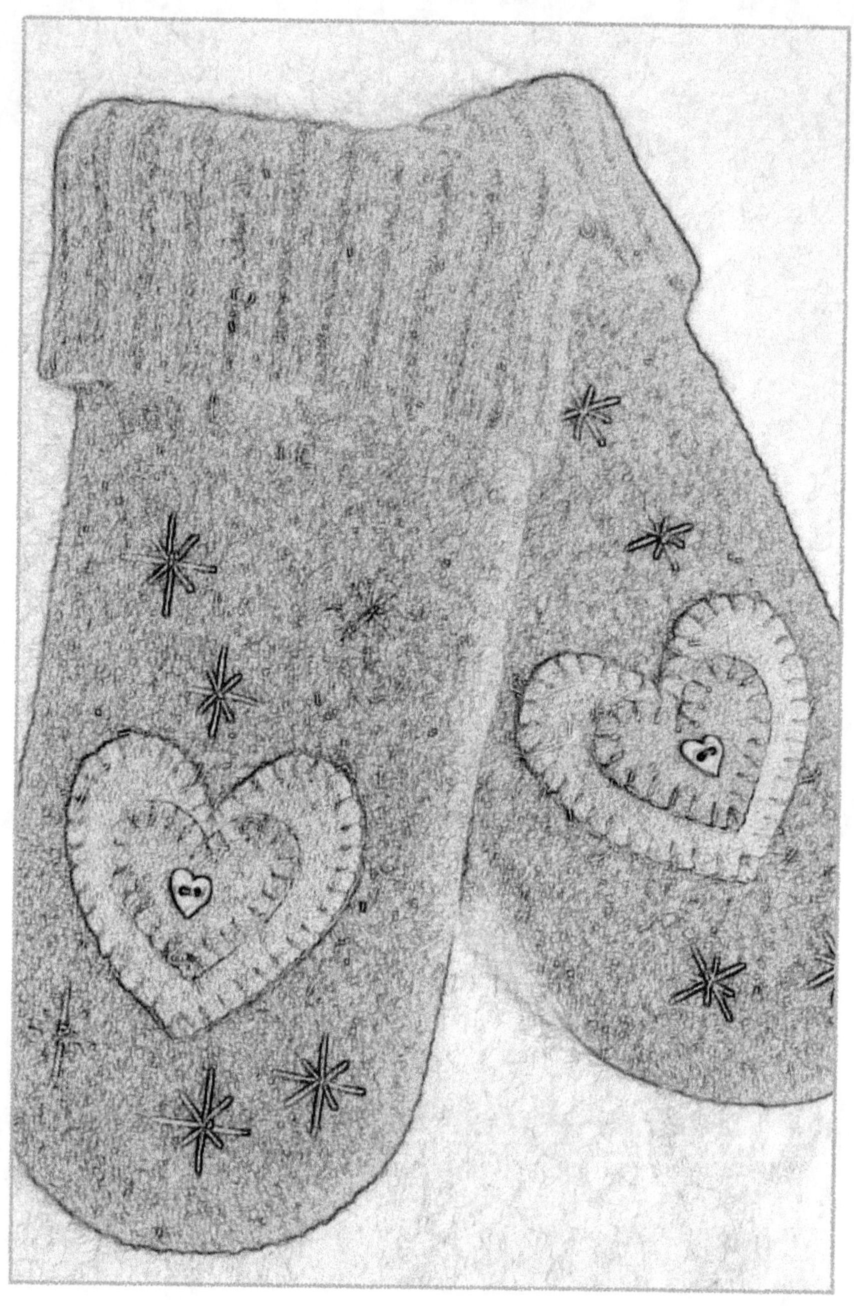

Amazing mazes

After lunch came the unpleasant task of putting their cold, soggy winter clothes back on. Each of the children took his or her scarf, hat, gloves, and jacket from the heavy wet pile on the table behind them. As they pushed their arms into their sleeves it felt like they were pushing into cold slime. Their hats were like jellyfish on their heads. Goosebumps covered their bodies as they stuck their fingers into gooey gloves. As soon as they were dressed they wanted to get moving so they could warm up again.

They walked over the wooden floor with the puddles where snow from people's boots had melted, and out the swinging doors. Snow was softly falling and everything around them was white. The sounds of children having skiing lessons and the engines of the pomas were muffled. After the warmth of the hut, the air was cold on their cheeks. Little snowflakes landed on their eyelashes and noses. The children hurried through the snow away from the ski slopes to the part of the mountain where they had been tobogganing in the morning. Tahlia walked closely behind her sister with her hand on Laurel's shoulder. The four parents came more slowly behind.

The children found some deep soft snow. "Let's make a maze through the snow!" suggested Leezah. Everyone agreed it was a great idea. On her hands and knees Leezah started scooping snow out of the way, making a path through the snow. The others followed her, each one making the path deeper and wider. Tahlia could tell by sound and feel where to dig and where to put the snow and she worked hard. Soon all of them were warm again, despite their wet clothes.

The children dug and scooped, making piles of snow along the edge of their paths through snow. Soon the paths were deep and long. They went in various directions. The children's clothes were wet from snow and sweat but they felt warm as they were working hard. When they had a maze of paths they decided to play chasings. So that Tahlia could join in safely they decided that no-one could stand up – they all had to move by crawling along the paths.

Laurel was 'in' first so she counted to twenty so the others could scramble off through the paths in the snow. Then she crawled as fast as she could, trying to find and catch someone. Up ahead she saw a red gumboot belonging to Leezah so she moved her knees and hands even faster. Soon Leezah's squeals and shrieks could be heard coming from a corner of the maze where she was trapped and tagged by Laurel. This was followed by: "One, two, three, four, five…" as Leezah counted so that Laurel had a chance to get away.

Hiding, and chasing each other through the snow was so fun that the children could not believe it when, a few hours later, they saw Rommy and Flip on the edge of the tunnel and heard Flip say "Five more minutes my little yetis. Then we need to get ready to go. The sun will set in about half an hour." There were groans and objections from all parts of the snow maze.

But, five minutes later, with red cheeks, and covered in dustings of snow, five sodden but happy children clambered out of their maze. Tahlia waited for Laurel to come to her and together they walked up the hill to their parents.

"So, dead boring eh?" asked Flip. "Never coming back here again?"

"Noooo!" cried the children. "We had so much fun." "Can we come back next weekend?" "Can Tahlia and Laurel come stay with us on the farm?" "Thank you so much for bringing us!"

Prunes in gloves

Back at the hut everyone changed out of their wet soggy ski clothes into a dry set of clothes. "Look at my fingers!" cried Olly as he pulled his hands out of the sodden gloves. His fingers were wrinkled like little pink prunes from being in the wet gloves all afternoon. "Mine too!" said Skye. Soon there was a circle of fifty pruney fingers being compared. Tahlia touched the hands of her friends to see if they felt the same as her own. The children also compared bruises. Everyone's knees were battered from crawling all afternoon. Skye-Maree had a bruise on her shoulder where Tahlia had accidentally kicked her while trying to get away. And Laurel and Olly had bumps on their heads where they had come around a corner in the maze in opposite directions. But the day had been very fun, and worth every bump!

The children didn't want to say goodbye to their new friends. Tahlia begged her mother to invite the Fitzgerald children to come and play at their house in Launceston. The parents swapped phone numbers and emails and promised to stay in touch. The children hugged goodbye. They also went to say goodbye and thank you to Magic who was packing away the skis, boots and poles that customers had returned after their day of skiing.

"You're off?" he said. "Come show me your goggle marks then." Olly went over to him. "Mmmm definitely the start of a good panda in the making here Olly," said Magic. "Keep working on it and we'll be able to welcome you to our panda family," he added, with a serious face.

"Ok," said Olly. "I will!"

The two families turned to leave the hut, clutching wet clothes and empty food bags. They started dropping hats and gloves before they even got to the door. Magic called out. "Come here I'll show you a trick I learned in the army." Magic showed them how to tuck their gloves and scarves and hats into the sleeves of their jackets so they only had two things to carry – their jackets and their ski pants.

"Thank you!"

The families walked down the snow-covered path to the car park. Without their ski clothes on, and with the sun setting, it was very cold so they had very quick goodbye hugs before jumping in their cars.   After Flip started the engine he put the heater on, but it took a while to heat up. Everyone was shivering as cold air blew into the car. Flip put the headlights on and started the careful drive winding down the mountain. Before they reached the top of Jacob's Ladder the heater was blowing warm air and everyone was feeling more comfortable.

Rommy handed out some apples and muesli bars she had left in the car especially for the trip home. These were quickly devoured. At the bottom of Jacob's Ladder Flip pulled over to remove the chains from the wheels. The children felt very sorry for him having to get out of the warm car into the cold darkness. But he quickly removed the chains and they continued their journey down the mountain. The children chattered and joked, reminding each other of some of the fun, funny, and scary, moments from the weekend on Ben Lomond. Laughing and telling stories with her siblings, even Skye-Maree forgot to get car sick.

When they arrived in Launceston they pulled into a bakery that stayed open late on Saturdays and Sundays especially to serve people coming in to town after being up the mountain. From the car, the children watched Rommy go into the brightly lit bakery full of bread, rolls and pastries. She bought loaves of fresh crusty bread to share, and filled their water bottles.

As they drove through the night they took it in turns to pull chunks of the fresh bread from the loaves, which filled their tummies. When all that was left of the bread was crumbs all over the seats and floor of the ute, the children sat back on their seats and watched the moon through the windows of the car. It seemed to be moving with them as they drove. Very soon, the only person awake was Flip.

But not for long.

A furry baby

Flip pulled abruptly over to the side of the road. The children were jolted forward and pulled back against their seats by their seatbelts. They opened their eyes sleepily and wondered where they were. Then they realized they were in the car. "Are we home Daddy?" asked Leezah from the middle of the back seat.

"No," said Flip in a distracted voice looking out the front window. "Not yet darling." He unlatched his seatbelt and opened his door. The winter night air was frosty as it flowed into the warm car. He shut the door behind himself. The headlights shone on the grass by the side of the road. Flip walked in the light of the headlights off the road and across the grass.

"Oh no!" said Leezah, looking through the front window. A wallaby was writhing on the side of the road.

Rommy joined Flip by the side of the road. They both bent over the injured animal. Rommy seemed to be touching its stomach.

Then she straightened up, with her arms crossed over her chest. Flip took the wallaby away from the headlights toward the bush. Leezah couldn't see what he was doing.

Soon Flip came back into the stream of light from the headlights. He wiped his hands on the wet grass, rubbed them together, wiped them on the grass again, then wiped them on his jeans. Flip opened the passenger door for Rommy and she climbed back into the ute. Then he shut the door and went around to the driver's side.

Flip reached into the lunch bag and passed Rommy a teatowel, then he helped her with her seatbelt. As Flip turned on the engine, and pulled back onto the road, Leezah asked: "What happened?"

Flip explained that the car ahead of them had hit a wallaby. "How mean!" said Skye-Maree. "No, not mean," said Flip. "It's easy to do. The wallabies jump out suddenly across the road. In the dark there's no warning. The driver wasn't going too fast. It was just unlucky."

Flip explained that the wallaby had been seriously hurt but not killed by the car ahead. So Flip had pulled over to check on it. Rommy, who was the Kellyton vet, agreed with Flip that the kindest thing to do would be to stop the pain of the wallaby by killing it quickly. But before they did, they checked its pouch, and found a mature joey in the pouch. The joey was not hurt. Flip took the mother wallaby to the bush and quickly brought an end to her suffering. Rommy was holding the joey in the tea towel, trying to keep it warm.

"Can I please see?" asked Olingah.

Rommy shifted the joey from her chest up to her shoulder so Olingah could see it from the back seat.

"Oh, it's so cute," said Skye-Maree. "May I hold it Mum?" Rommy nodded and turned to pass the joey to her daughter.

"Oh! I want to hold it!" cried Olly, making the joey jerk with fear at the sudden loud voice.

Skye-Maree took the small animal wrapped in cloth from her mother and lowered it carefully onto her lap.

"That's not fair!" said Olly. "I asked first! I want to hold the joey!"

Rommy twisted herself in her seat so she could see Olingah sitting directly behind her. Olingah looked very tired. The joey also looked very frightened. Loud voices and noises would scare the joey even more.

"Olly," said Rommy gently, "please speak quietly or you will scare the wallaby."

Olingah started to cry. He whined, "Why does Skye-Maree get all the good things? I wanted to hold the joey."

Rommy explained that the joey would need some care for several weeks and everyone would get a chance to hold it. But Olly was not listening.   "Olingah Giachery William!" said Rommy softly but firmly. "Please show me the shining gem of patience and selflessness!"

Olingah turned away from Rommy, Leezah and Skye-Maree. He was feeling very frustrated and cross. He put his head back on the seat and looked out the window. A few minutes later he was fast asleep again. And on Skye-Maree's lap, so was the joey.

Mad dogs

Flip pulled in to the farm house at Fellowship Farm. The only light was the night light shining on the path that ran up the side of the house to the back door. The rest of the house was pitch black. The chickens were fast asleep in their hen house. The farm dogs were sleeping up at the shed. The pigs in the sty were snuggled into the straw. All across the fields was darkness. And in their kennel at the back of the house lay the pet dogs: Fizz, Flea and Flex.

As the sleepy family waddled up the path to the back of the house, the dogs woke and started to jump around excitedly in the back yard. Skye-Maree passed the joey to Rommy, freeing her hands to pat the excited and very hungry dogs. Leezah hurried up the steps of the verandah to the bin that held their food. She filled their bowls and dropped them on the grass near the kennel. They ran to gobble it up. The family had only planned to be away for one day so they had not organized for anyone to feed the animals.

Even the excited dogs could not really wake Olingah, who shuffled up the stairs of the verandah, through the kitchen and living room, into the bedroom. He flopped onto his bed. He curled up like a wombat under his doona and fell straight back to sleep.

Rommy wrapped the joey in a warm jumper and put it in a box in the living room. Flip brought the ski clothes in from the car and put a load in the washing machine. Leezah and Skye-Maree finished patting the dogs and came inside. The house was cold and dark. Rommy lit the fire in the fireplace and turned on the lamps. After hot showers Leezah and Skye-Maree came out by the fire in their pajamas for evening prayers. It was already past their bedtime and they had school the next day.

"Thank you for a wonderful weekend," said Leezah as Rommy brushed and plaited her hair for bed.

"Our pleasure treasure," replied Flip who had a curly-haired daughter on his lap.

"What will happen to the joey Mummy?" asked Skye-Maree.

"Well it's quite big already so I think there is a good chance it will survive. We can care for it here for a few weeks. Then set it free in the bush."

"It might get lonely by itself here. Maybe I should take it to school tomorrow?" suggested Skye-Maree hopefully.

"Mmm, I think it would be better if I take it to work with me," smiled Rommy.

"Ok," said Skye-Maree with disappointment.

When Leezah's plaits were finished Flip took the guitar out of its case. The family sat reverently, then started to sing: "Where there is love, nothing is too much trouble, and there's always time." After several more prayers, it was time for bed. Leezah and Skye-Maree kissed their mum and dad good night.

In the bedroom they passed their brother, the little wombat, burrowed down in his doonah. Leezah climbed the creaky ladder to the top bunk and Skye-Maree climbed into the bottom bunk. At first it felt like they would never get to sleep. "Hey Leezah," whispered Skye-Maree, "remember when we started skiing and we kept falling off the pomas?"

"Yes, and remember when you went charging down the mountain and fell over and your ski slid all the way down by itself?"

"Yes, and remember when ...."

The whispered 'remember whens' continued for a long time until they were interrupted by the voice of Flip who appeared at the doorway: "Remember when two wicked, evil, and naughty girls stayed up talking too late and their father had to glue their eyes and mouths shut?"

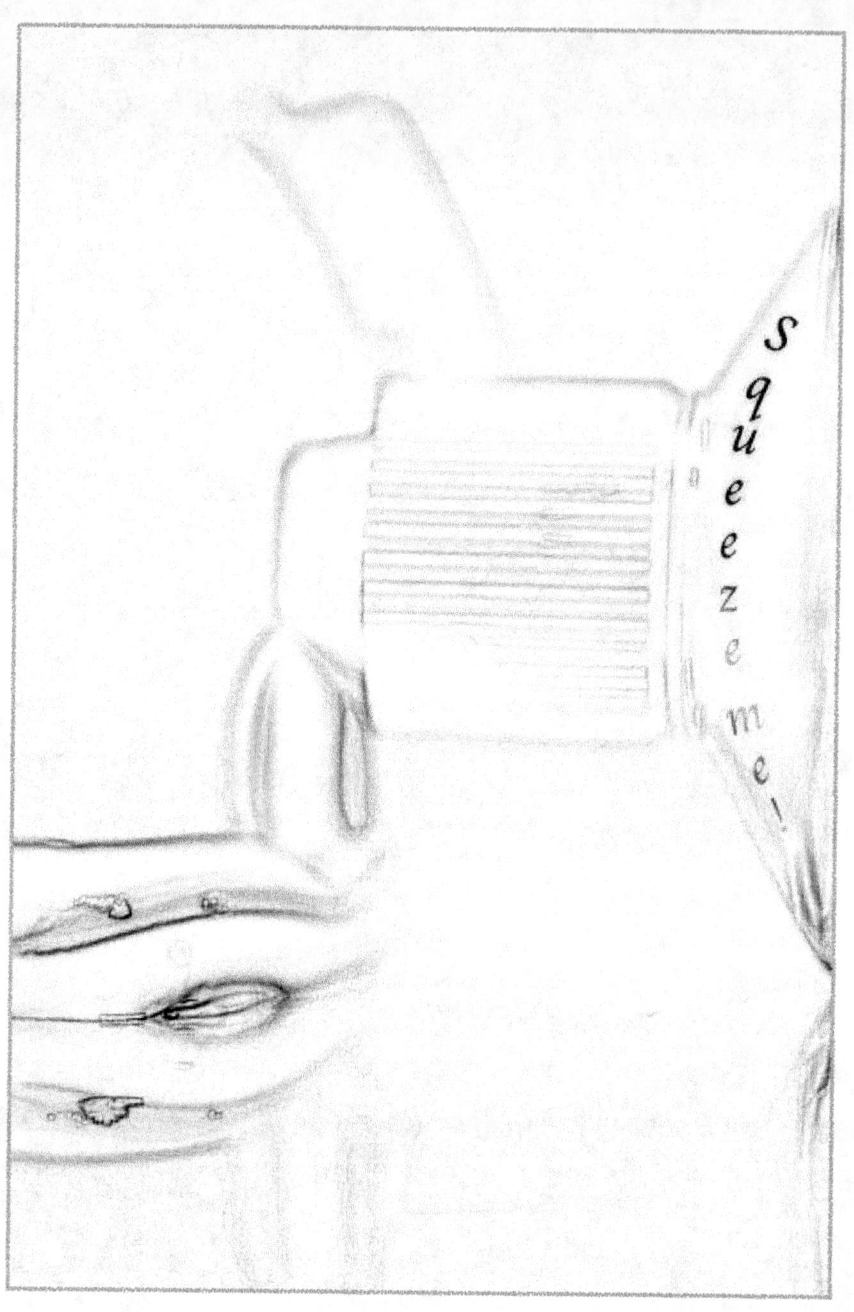
Squeeze me!

Bread and unity

When the Fitzgerald children woke early the next morning they immediately felt two things. Their bodies felt sore – all weekend they had been using muscles they didn't usually use. And, they were very very hungry! After a busy day in the snow they had just had bread for dinner. Their tummies were gurgling. When they came out of the bedroom, Rommy was setting and lighting the fire.

"I'm starving Mum!" said Olingah.

"I'm not surprised," said Rommy. "Shall we have our physical breakfast before our spiritual breakfast this morning?" There were no objections.

Flip cooked up a frying pan full of eggs and filled the grill with bacon. Olingah was responsible for making toast and slicing tomatoes, while the girls set the table. Normally they had cereal for breakfast on school days but this morning everyone was hungry.

When the food was on the table and everyone was ready to start eating, Rommy said quietly, "Thank You Baha'u'llah".

"Yes," said Flip, "Thank You for this beautiful food for this beautiful family."

"I am soo hungry!" said Skye-Maree, as they started to eat.

Flip asked, "Why do you think we are so hungry this morning?"

Leezah said "Because we were in the snow all day and only had bread for dinner?"

"Two hundred points to the girl in the spotty pajamas!" grinned Flip. Then he added, "You know there are children in Afghanistan who eat a kind of bread for every meal nearly all year round."

"With nothing else?" asked Olingah

"Nothing else. And winters in Afghanistan are very cold. Many of the children have nowhere to live, nothing but bread to eat, and very little to wear."

"Why?"

"Because there is no unity," answered Rommy.

"So, if we don't have unity will you only give us bread to eat?" asked Olingah.

"No, that's not what I mean," laughed Rommy. "Disunity leads to war and conflict. War hurts and kills people. War damages farms and homes. Children and families have to run away from where they live and hide in forests. Lots of money is wasted on guns. Those are some of the ways disunity makes people poor, cold and hungry."

"I wish there was no war!" said Leezah. "I wish I could stop war."

After breakfast was finished the family worked together to clear the table. Rommy prepared a bottle of Wombaroo milk for the joey. The children were keen to have a turn feeding the joey. Rommy reminded them that they needed to have their morning prayers, feed the farm animals, and get ready for school, all before the school bus arrived. They realized they didn't have much time and hurried off to the bathroom to brush their teeth.

In the bathroom Leezah reached for the toothpaste right at the same time as Skye-Maree. "I had it first," said Leezah and tried to pull it out of Skye-Maree's hand. Skye held on tighter and pulled back.

"Let go!" cried Leezah. "I. Had. It. First!" She yanked the tube from Skye-Maree's grasp. Just then, toothpaste shot up into the air and into Skye-Maree's eye and hair. She started to scream. Flip came into the bathroom. He helped her lean over the sink so he could scoop handfuls of water into her eye to stop the stinging.

Leezah felt very bad. She was sorry that Skye's eye was hurting. And she was sorry she had grabbed the toothpaste. She was sorry they had disunity. She started to cry. "Sorry sister," she said. Skye's eye was clean now, but it was red and stinging. She went with Flip into the living room to sit on the couch until it stopped hurting. Leezah went and sat with her. She thought about how a few minutes ago she was wishing she could stop the fighting in the world, and then she was fighting with her very own sister! When Skye's eye was feeling better the family decided to have their morning prayers. Leezah sang: "So powerful is the light of unity that it can illuminate the whole earth." She promised herself she would try harder to be a cause of unity.

Lunch orders

The red school bus pulled up at the front of Fellowship Farm. Ms Rowbottom opened the door of the bus with her big lever. The children climbed on. "Good morning Ms Rowbottom," they called as they passed the bus driver. Ms Rowbottom grunted, pulled the lever to shut the door, and drove off down the road. On the way to the town the bus stopped at other farms to pick up the children.

The children were very excited to share the news of the ski trip with their friends on the bus. They were also excited because they were having a special treat for lunch. Instead of making their lunch at home, they each had some money to buy food from the school canteen. Olingah knew exactly what he would order: a hot cheese roll and a pineapple poppa. Skye-Marie wanted a mini pizza and an orange poppa. And Leezah wanted a pastie with sauce and a chocolate milk. No-one had time to make lunch that morning as they had spent more time than usual on breakfast.

When each of them got to their classrooms they put their money in a brown paper bag and wrote their lunch order on the outside. Lunch orders were very rare and they loved them.

When the bell for lunchtime rang the Fitzgerald children ran to the canteen to line up for their hot lunch. Their tummies were rumbling. Olingah was second in line when the canteen opened. He took his hot cheese roll and his poppa to the lunch area. His friends gathered around hoping for a bite. Olingah generously swapped a bite of his roll for a bit of a peanut butter sandwich with one friend. Then he had a bite of another friend's muesli bar in exchange for a bit of his roll. And then he ate the rest himself. He loved the way the cheese was gooey and stretchy. The first mouthful nearly burned his tongue and he had to open his mouth and puff and pant to cool it off. But after he finished, it felt warm in his tummy.

On the other side of the lunch area Olingah could see Leezah licking tomato sauce off her fingers. Skye-Maree had finished her poppa and had blown air into it. She put it on the ground and jumped on it making a bang. Then she put the empty box in the bin.

It was very hard to concentrate on school work that afternoon. Instead of listening to the teacher Olingah was remembering whizzing down the mountain on his toboggan. Instead of reading her book Skye-Maree was twisting and turning on her skis, rushing toward the bottom of the mountain. Instead of working on her sums Leezah was remembering getting up in the dark with the snow falling to make a snow-woman.

It would be a while before the children would get back to Ben Lomond but that was because there were other adventures to be had.

But that is another story.

Chapter images courtesy of Flickr.com

1. Anthony Joch
   https://www.flickr.com/photos/ajoch/

2. Rock Pigeon
   https://www.flickr.com/photos/woodpigeon/

3. Stratman
   https://www.flickr.com/photos/stratman2/

4. Colin Lee
   https://www.flickr.com/photos/colin-d-lee/

5. Cheryl "FeltSewGood"
   https://www.flickr.com/photos/feltsewgood/

6. Size Barnes
   https://www.flickr.com/photos/therealpictures/

7. Dave Taylor
   https://www.flickr.com/photos/54919275@N08/

8. Stock image

9. Karen Anderson
   https://www.flickr.com/photos/k4wea/

10. Michelangela

Fellowship Farm

Volume 1: Books 1 - 3

Leezah, Skye-Maree and Olingah Fitzgerald live with their parents on Fellowship Farm. In the first book of the Fellowship Farm series, you will meet the children and learn about their daily activities on the farm. There is a lot to be done each day: pillow fights, morning prayers, pig feeding and school bus riding. They help their dad feed the cows, add stickers to their virtues poster and learn to deal with bullies.

Then you will join the Fitzgerald children on their many adventures with puppies, snake bites, treasure hunts, bonfires, camping by the sea, and tree houses. And as they go they sometimes practice their virtues, and sometimes forget...

Suitable for independent readers aged 8-12 years; parent-read from six years. Order online from print-on-demand services, and digitally from the iBookstore or Kindle.

Fellowship Farm

Volume 2: Books 4 - 6

Leezah, Skye-Maree and Olingah Fitzgerald live with their parents on Fellowship Farm. In the first volume of the Fellowship Farm series, you met the children and learned about their daily activities on the farm.

In this the second volume the Fitzgerald children are visited by their cousins, Nick and Anisa. Together they travel by horse and cart to the market, attend the 19 Day Feast, go camping, find a pirate map and treasure, as well as experience the intensity of crisis and victory when Olingah's life is put in serious danger.

Suitable for independent readers aged 8-12 years; parent-read from six years. Order online from print-on-demand services, and digitally from the iBookstore or Kindle.

Fellowship Farm

Volume 3: Books 7 - 9

In this, the third volume of stories about Leezah, Skye-Maree and Olingah Fitzgerald who live with their parents on Fellowship Farm, the children set out with joy to go blackberry picking.

But an unexpected turn of events at the river makes them fear for the lives of their puppies. Ayyám-i-Há follows with serving, teaching, gifts, treasure hunts as well as the challenge of bullying for Skye-Maree. After Ayyám-i-Há comes an opportunity to visit their eccentric Uncle Jack who takes them to the chocolate factory, aquatic centre and gives them many other treats both spiritual and edible!

Suitable for independent readers aged 8-12 years; parent-read from six years. Order online from print-on-demand services, and digitally from the iBookstore or Kindle.

Fellowship Farm

Volume 4: Books 10 - 12

In the fourth volume of stories about Leezah, Skye-Maree and Olingah Fitzgerald of Fellowship Farm they prepare for the annual Naw Ruz Mahta River Boat Race. There are some unexpected hitches.

Skye-Maree and Olingah learn about loyalty and sacrifice as they work out how to

respond to the challenges they face. Soon after Naw Ruz winter sets in and the family rug up and head for the ski slopes. Along the way they experience the life-threatening danger of losing unity, the challenge of learning to ski, the power of prayer, and patience in the face of frustration. They meet funny Magic, the back to front panda, and suffer some bruises. Their patience is well rewarded when their parents announce that a dear wish of the children is to be fulfilled.

Suitable for independent readers aged 8-12 years; parent-read from six years. Order online from print-on-demand services, and digitally from the iBookstore or Kindle.

Unity in Diversity

This brightly illustrated picture book contains five simple stories for young readers. They foster an understanding of the oneness of the human race and celebrate its diversity within that unity.

Likening the human race to various colored cotton in a woven cloth, various fruits on the tree of life, stars in the heavens, members of one body, and different notes in one perfect chord, the stories use the concrete to teach the abstract.

Young readers will enjoy the bright colors and simple text as they develop their understanding of the unity and diversity of the human race.

Ideal for children aged 4-8 years.
Order online from print-on-demand services, and digitally from the iBookstore. Translated into French, Portuguese, Romanian, Tetum, and Mongolian.

The Big Story

The Big Story explains the way in which the divinely ordained and guided process that has brought human beings into existence has taken place gradually over time and space. It shows that the concepts of evolution and creation are not mutually exclusive.

Science and religion are shown to be two windows on one reality, two knowledge systems that when properly understood, function as one cohesive whole.

This book is most suitable for readers 14 years and older. Younger readers will enjoy the bright and informative illustrations but will require support to understand the text.

Suitable for independent readers aged 14+ years; with assistance from 12+. Order online from print-on-demand services, and digitally from the iBookstore.

Dr Melanie Lotfali

Author of The Fitzgeralds of Fellowship Farm series and Unity in Diversity series.

Melanie Lotfali PhD is a graduate of the Australian College of Journalism in Professional Writing for Children. She is the author of eighteen books of fiction and non-fiction for children and the illustrator of five.

Melanie has taught spiritual education classes for children for the past twenty years in five countries and is currently an active animator and trainer of animators for the Junior Youth Spiritual Empowerment Program. She is a qualified counselor and classroom teacher, and for over six years facilitated violence prevention and respectful relationships programs in high schools.

Much of her childhood was spent on the farms, beaches and mountains of Tasmania, where the Fellowship Farm series is set. As an adult she spent four years in Siberia and four years in East Timor as a pioneer.

She currently lives in Lismore, Australia, with her family.

Michael Cohen

Author of The Big Story and publisher of all Michelangela books.

Michael Cohen graduated as a Computer Systems Engineer in 1990 and worked for many years in software design and

informations systems. He changed careers in 2008 to become a registered nurse working in the area of Mental Health and Alcohol & Other Drugs.

Michael has been a keen participant in and advocate of the programs offered by **The Foundation for the Application and Teaching of the Sciences** (FUNDAEC) and **Institute for Studies in Global Prosperity** (ISGP). He strives to contribute to processes and discourses leading to the progress of humankind toward a world society characterized by unity, justice and equity. A fundamental premise of Michael's worldview is that true science and true religion are necessarily in harmony, indeed are two windows on one reality. His writing seeks to promote understanding of this liberating concept and to contribute to a civilization that is ever advancing materially and spiritually.

He currently lives in Lismore, Australia, with his family.

Michelangela

website www.michelangela.com.au
email info@michelangela.com.au

To receive Michelangela's occasional product announcements please visit our website and enter your email address and name via the subscribe button

www.ingramcontent.com/pod-product-compliance
Lightning Source LLC
Chambersburg PA
CBHW070606120726
47909CB00007B/2463